THE CYCLOPS

John Blackburn was born in 1923 in tl
the second son of a clergyman. Blackburn attended Haileybury College near London beginning in 1937, but his education was interrupted by the onset of World War II; the shadow of the war, and that of Nazi Germany, would later play a role in many of his works. He served as a radio officer during the war in the Mercantile Marine from 1942 to 1945, and resumed his education afterwards at Durham University, earning his bachelor's degree in 1949. Blackburn taught for several years after that, first in London and then in Berlin, and married Joan Mary Clift in 1950. Returning to London in 1952, he took over the management of Red Lion Books.

It was there that Blackburn began writing, and the immediate success in 1958 of his first novel, *A Scent of New-Mown Hay*, led him to take up a career as a writer full time. He and his wife also maintained an antiquarian bookstore, a secondary career that would inform some of Blackburn's work, including the bibliomystery *Blue Octavo* (1963). *A Scent of New-Mown Hay* typified the approach that would come to characterize Blackburn's twenty-eight novels, which defied easy categorization in their unique and compelling mixture of the genres of science fiction, horror, mystery, and thriller. Many of Blackburn's best novels came in the late 1960s and early 1970s, with a string of successes that included the classics *A Ring of Roses* (1965), *Children of the Night* (1966), *Nothing but the Night* (1968; adapted for a 1973 film starring Christopher Lee and Peter Cushing), *Devil Daddy* (1972) and *Our Lady of Pain* (1974). Somewhat unusually for a popular horror writer, Blackburn's novels were not only successful with the reading public but also won widespread critical acclaim: the *Times Literary Supplement* declared him 'today's master of horror' and compared him with the Grimm Brothers, while the *Penguin Encyclopedia of Horror and the Supernatural* regarded him as 'certainly the best British novelist in his field' and the *St James Guide to Crime & Mystery Writers* called him 'one of England's best practicing novelists in the tradition of the thriller novel'.

By the time Blackburn published his final novel in 1985, much of his work was already out of print, an inexplicable neglect that continued until Valancourt began republishing his novels in 2013. John Blackburn died in 1993.

By John Blackburn

A Scent of New-Mown Hay (1958)*

A Sour Apple Tree (1958)

Broken Boy (1959)*

Dead Man Running (1960)

The Gaunt Woman (1962)

Blue Octavo (1963)*

Colonel Bogus (1964)

The Winds of Midnight (1964)

A Ring of Roses (1965)*

Children of the Night (1966)*

The Flame and the Wind (1967)*

Nothing but the Night (1968)*

The Young Man from Lima (1968)

Bury Him Darkly (1969)*

Blow the House Down (1970)

The Household Traitors (1971)*

Devil Daddy (1972)*

For Fear of Little Men (1972)

Deep Among the Dead Men (1973)

Our Lady of Pain (1974)*

Mister Brown's Bodies (1975)

The Face of the Lion (1976)*

The Cyclops Goblet (1977)*

Dead Man's Handle (1978)

The Sins of the Father (1979)

A Beastly Business (1982)*

The Book of the Dead (1984)

The Bad Penny (1985)*

* Available or forthcoming from Valancourt Books

JOHN BLACKBURN

THE CYCLOPS GOBLET

With a new introduction by

GREG GBUR

VALANCOURT BOOKS

The Cyclops Goblet by John Blackburn
First published London: Jonathan Cape, 1977
First Valancourt Books edition 2014

Published by Valancourt Books, Richmond, Virginia
Publisher & Editor: James D. Jenkins
20th Century Series Editor: Simon Stern, University of Toronto
http://www.valancourtbooks.com

ISBN 978-1-939140-88-3 (*trade paperback*)
Also available as an electronic book.

Set in Dante MT 11/13.6
Cover by M. S. Corley

INTRODUCTION

For those who are only familiar with John Blackburn's most famous books, his 1977 novel *The Cyclops Goblet* will be a pleasant surprise and a significant departure from his usual fare. Unlike Blackburn's best-known work, which features heroic British agents fighting to stop horrific, even apocalyptic, threats, *The Cyclops Goblet* shares the darkly humorous and twisted exploits of a petty criminal as he tries to pull off a massive heist – and keep himself alive.

By 1977, the prolific John Blackburn (1923-1993) had been an author for nearly twenty years, producing about a score of novels in the process. The success of his first – *A Scent of New-Mown Hay*, published in 1958 – gave him the freedom to quit his job as the director of Red Lion Books in London and pursue his writing nearly full time. He would, however, manage an antiquarian bookstore with his wife, an occupation that also would inspire several of his works.

Blackburn's fiction can broadly be divided into tales of horror and more conventional thrillers. Though his horror novels are arguably quite distinct, many of them follow the broad outline used with great effect in *A Scent of New-Mown Hay*. In these stories, a mysterious and deadly malady strikes, threatening widespread death and even the possible destruction of humanity. A small number of brave and intelligent heroes recognize the danger and seek to halt the plague, in the process uncovering a sinister conspiracy driving it. Blackburn is known for using a recurring cast of characters in his books, including the clever and cynical General Kirk of British Intelligence and the brilliant bacteriologist Marcus Levin.

By the 1970s, it seems that Blackburn was interested in shaking up his writing somewhat, and in the 1973 novel *Deep Among the Dead Men* he introduced a character of a quite different calibre. Bill Easter is a scoundrel: a former gangster, a bodyguard, and a perennial con-man who is always on the lookout for the big score. He is a traditional anti-hero, a protagonist who lacks morality or any sense of altruism. In a further departure from Blackburn's previous writing, Bill Easter colourfully narrates his own adventures in the first person.

In *Deep Among the Dead Men*, Easter travels to the (fictional) West African country of Leonia. His mission? To claim a fortune in treasure sunken off the coast. The catch? Before the treasure can be recovered, the vicious dictator of Leonia must be assassinated, a task that Easter is more than willing to carry out. By the end of the novel, Easter and new partner-in-crime Peggy Tey have sailed from Leonia with a sizable fortune in one of the former dictator's boats. However, by the beginning of *Mister Brown's Bodies* (1975), they have lost their vessel in a crash and are adrift in a lifeboat far off the African coast. They are rescued by a ship with a particularly peculiar passenger list: nine notorious and wanted criminals who had supposedly been executed in Leonia not long ago. The ship travels to England, and Bill and Peggy ironically end up working to prevent a particularly destructive assassination attempt.

At the beginning of *The Cyclops Goblet*, Bill and Peggy are down and out and struggling to pay the rent in London. They are contacted unexpectedly by Colonel Wellington Booth, the leader of a fascistic British nationalist movement, and asked to help break into an impregnable vault and steal the Danemere Treasure, a priceless Renaissance dinner set that is reputed to have been cursed by the demented artist who created it. What follows is a series of twists and turns, crosses and double-crosses, as Bill works with and against his partners in crime, sometimes simultaneously, in a quest to retrieve the treasure. In the process, Bill and Peggy will have to solve the riddles of the last caretaker of the collection and uncover its true horrible secret.

The Cyclops Goblet is, in fact, part treasure hunt and part 'caper' story, the latter type being particularly popular in that era. Like all capers, the quest for the Danemere Treasure involves ingenious schemes and multiple betrayals, leaving the reader guessing until the very end. The novel is, in fact, unique, as it is arguably Blackburn's only true heist story, naturally raising the question of what inspired him to write it. Though Blackburn did not leave any correspondence or give any interviews about his muses, an obvious suspect in the case of the *Goblet* is the quirky British movie *The Italian Job* (1969), starring Michael Caine, Noel Coward and Benny Hill. In the film, an eclectic collection of mobsters and thieves scheme to steal $4 million in gold bullion and spirit it out of Italy. *The Cyclops Goblet* has the same dark humour as the movie, and other similarities can be found. For example: in *The Italian Job*, the criminals must break a needed compatriot out of prison; in *The Cyclops Goblet*, the conspirators must break a woman with important information out of a psychiatric hospital! Blackburn's story, however, has a much more sinister denouement.

Another possible inspiration – and we must admit that we are merely speculating here – is the fantastic 1964 burglary of the American Natural History Museum of New York, popularly known as the 'Heist of the Century'. A number of precious gems were stolen, including the Star of India, a 563.35-carat star sapphire. The crime was perpetrated by three men, led by Jack Roland Murphy – a scoundrel who would likely earn the respect of Bill Easter. Murphy and his team had a much easier time than Easter, however. A preliminary casing of the museum showed that the alarm system was non-functional and, incredibly, a second-floor window leading into the jewel room was left open to aid in ventilation. Furthermore, the burglars discovered that the alarm on the Star of India's jewel case also had a dead battery. This should be contrasted with the protection on the Danemere Treasure in *The Cyclops Goblet*, which is described as perfectly impregnable. It is worth noting that almost all of the jewels stolen in the 'Heist of the Century' were recovered, with the exception of a diamond known as the Eagle Diamond, which is assumed to have been cut into smaller pieces and sold off.

The Cyclops Goblet was well received, as reviews of the time indicate. Writing in the *Guardian*, Norman Shrapnel described the book as follows:

> This is Gothic diablerie with a smile – a very nasty smile, as though a Charles Addams character had escaped from his picture and perpetrated an elaborate practical joke in prose.

> But the story, if you can stand it, does take you along – all the way to [a] remote Scottish island where unspeakable things are spoken of.

Writing in the *Observer*, Maurice Richardson summarized the novel as 'Another semi-surrealist pseudo-Gothic adventure of Bill Easter', and gave the most concise review possible: 'Read on if you can; I could.'

This positive reception of Bill Easter's antics no doubt helped motivate Blackburn to continue writing about him. Bill Easter would later feature in *A Beastly Business* (1982), where his path would cross at last with General Charles Kirk. The two of them would take their final bow together in Blackburn's last published novel, *The Bad Penny*, in 1985.

One other part of *The Cyclops Goblet* is worth highlighting for its historical interest. The 'remote Scottish island' mentioned in Shrapnel's review is called Alt-na-Shan in the novel and is unofficially known as 'Anthrax Island', having been contaminated by biological warfare experimentation. It is based on the very real Gruinard Island off the Scottish coast, including its dangerous contamination. In 1942, the British military used the island to test the feasibility of using anthrax as a bioweapon and the danger of it being used against them as well. As a result of these tests, the island was rendered uninhabitable and it was deemed too costly to decontaminate.

Proving once again the adage that 'truth is stranger than fiction', the real Gruinard Island became the motivation for a bioterrorism attack on the United Kingdom in 1981. A group known only as 'Dark Harvest Commando' announced to the newspapers that they had acquired anthrax-tainted soil from the island and would leave it 'at appropriate points' to terrorize the government and the public into a proper decontamination of the island. Only two such packages were ever found, and only the first was found to contain anthrax. Apparently without spurring from the 'Commandos', the Crown finally made an effort to clean Gruinard Island in 1986, and in 1990 the island was declared safe and resold back to its original owners – at the price of £500.

The inclusion of such a sinister island, and one contaminated with disease at that, shows that *The Cyclops Goblet* is still very much a John Blackburn novel. It is a nice balance of humour and horror and highlights how Blackburn could broaden his writing style while remaining true to his origins.

Greg Gbur

December 29, 2013

Greg Gbur is an associate professor of physics and optical science at the University of North Carolina at Charlotte. He writes the long-running blog 'Skulls in the Stars', which discusses classic horror fiction, physics and the history of science, as well as the curious intersections between the three topics. His science writing has recently been featured in 'The Best Science Writing Online 2012', published by Scientific American. He has previously introduced several other John Blackburn titles for Valancourt Books.

THE CYCLOPS GOBLET

for Hugh Lamb

I

Bank robbers, blackmailers and burglars, extortionists, forgers and perverts. I've met some prize villains during my career and till recently I thought I'd rubbed shoulders with the pick of the hemlock harvest. I've also been pally with two professional assassins and a bungling amateur murderer. The last was a pathetic little chap who added arsenic to one of Messrs Heinz 57 Varieties and fed the mixture to a rich aunt. Aunty died satisfactorily, but the fool tried to dispose of her in a wooden barrel filled with acid and the attempt failed. The timbers perished before the corpse was completely dissolved and quite literally spilled the beans.

Yes, I thought I'd sampled the broth of hell's cauldron, but how ruddy wrong I was. My former associates were merely crooks and nutcases. They only gained fame because of their crimes, and not one of them had ever been invited to a Buckingham Palace tea-party. The worst human beings I have ever encountered were celebrities. Respected household names, acclaimed by the public and wined and dined by royalty. I can't list them in order of rottenness. They were all completely rotten.

So let's take them in descending order of age. A Church of England bishop, who'd got himself elected president of an emergent African republic. A retired army colonel with more decorations than the Corps of Commissionaires and several dramatic wounds suffered in defence of his country's honour. The lady wife of said colonel, who'd been awarded an Olympic medal for horsemanship and would gouge out your eyes and call back for the sockets if you gave her the chance. An eminent doctor of medicine, who had isolated, but failed to tame, an objectionable disease. An American billionaire, who'd made his fortune by honest toil and spent it in the service of art. Those were the real baddies, and God help Lucifer when he gets lumbered with them.

Life had been hard before the summons arrived. Peggy Tey,

my common-law wife, had a job modelling outsize corsets and nobody was more suitable. Peg enjoys displaying her charms and she weighs fifteen stone in the buff. But the work wasn't regular, and I was contributing nothing because we'd been abroad for some time and had lost touch. My underworld contacts had either retired on their ill-gotten gains, fled the country or been lodged behind bars. A pen-pusher at the Ministry of Employment had offered me a selection of menial tasks, but the answer was, 'No thank you.' Bill Easter might be poor, but he had his pride and his price. I wasn't going to drive a bus, dole out parking-tickets, or sweep tube stations with a bunch of West Indians.

All the same, something had to be done because the wolves were closing in on the sleigh. Our landlord had applied for an eviction order, the debts were piling up, and life was bloody miserable. Peg and I were paupers and the only things we didn't lack were food and drink. Peggy's employers had to keep her weight stable and there was always a nourishing tuck-in after the corset parades. Nor is it difficult to obtain a buckshee meal if you're blessed with charm and courage, and I possess both.

I'm not referring to charity, of course; Sisters of Mercy handouts, or soup kitchens for the needy. The trick is to go to a good restaurant when it's crowded and there's no vacant table. Stare around as though you're looking for a friend and then sit down beside some solitary character and start a conversation with him. Defer to him and flatter him and, provided you play your cards well, he'll respond before you've asked his opinion of the wine list. You'll hear about his wife, or his piles, or the responsibilities of his job, and the waiters will soon believe that he's your host. Nobody will suspect a thing when you say that you're popping round the corner to buy a brand of cigarettes the restaurant doesn't stock and will be back in a jiffy. The fun only starts when the jiffy turns out to be *never*. The trouble begins after the new-found chum finishes his coffee and is presented with a double bill.

No, it's not difficult to eat on the house, though there's an element of risk which ruins the appetite. But our family fortunes had to be restored and Peg and I were discussing several possibilities when the phone interrupted us.

A surprising sound, because we'd had a disconnection notice a week ago, and as I went into the hall and lifted the receiver I expected to hear some post-office clerk demanding payment.

'Is that Mr Easter? Mr William Easter, who cohabits with a woman named Margaret Tey?' The approach was insolent and the caller had an arrogant huntin', shootin' and fishin' accent. But he didn't sound like a clerk or a debt-collector, so I admitted my identity and asked him his business.

'Urgent business. I've had a lot of trouble locating you, Mr Easter.' There was an open rebuke in the statement as though I was deliberately responsible for his trouble. 'We knew that you and Mrs Tey were living in London, but your name is not listed in the directory and the young person on the inquiry switchboard was as inefficient as such gels usually are.'

Quite right on the second point. The number was still listed in the name of a former tenant: Miss Gloria Fledgling. Another young person, though she looked about seventy and was being treated for heroin addiction.

'However, we've run you to earth at last, so let me introduce myself. I am Lesley Wellington Booth.' The introduction was made with a deal of pride which changed to petulance when I remained silent. 'Surely Wellington Booth conveys something to you, Mr Easter?'

It conveyed several things. The victor at Waterloo and a famous public school. A gin manufacturer, an American shipping company and old General Booth who founded the Salvation Army. Familiar names on their own, but not when joined together. I told Mr Wellington Booth that I couldn't place him or remember where we'd met.

'Not *Mr*.' Indignation rattled the receiver. 'This is Lady Lesley Wellington Booth speaking, and naturally we haven't met.' Her Ladyship made it clear that we moved in different circles and she had no desire to meet me socially. 'But we do share a close and trusted friend. That is why I have to see you, so may I have your address please?'

She damn well couldn't. Not till I knew who the mutual buddy was, because I hadn't got any close friends and I trusted no one.

What I had got was a legion of avaricious creditors and I didn't want them to know our whereabouts.

'I cannot divulge the person's name on the telephone, Mr Easter. The matter is extremely confidential and we might be overheard.' Lady Lesley was right again. Peggy and I shared a party line and the other subscriber was old and bored and sometimes listened in to our conversations. I'd often heard wheezy breathing through the earpiece. 'I will give you a hint though, Mr Easter. Your friend has a fondness for gin fizz.'

'You mean that he *had* a fondness for it.' I knew whom she was referring to, but the man wasn't a friend. He was a fat, self-seeking conniver, a Judas who'd betrayed me on three occasions, but there wouldn't be a fourth betrayal. The gin-swilling bastard had played one phoney ace too many and met his just deserts. A mob of disgruntled blacks had beaten him to pulp and strung his carcass from a lamp standard. I'd enjoyed reading details of the execution, which was widely reported by the press. The *Daily Globe* had described the brute as a TRUE CHRISTIAN MARTYR. The *Evening Echo* compared him to Saint Stephen, David Livingstone and Albert Schweitzer.

'Yes, the poor man is dead, Mr Easter, though I use the word *poor* in the sense of unhappy.' Lady Lesley's rasping, yah-yah voice became wheedling and I waited for her bait. A carrot to tempt the donkey forward. 'Our friend probably died a millionaire and you are named as one of his beneficiaries. It is in your own interest to collaborate with us, so will you please tell me where we can find you.'

How I wish I'd rejected the carrot then and there. If only I'd slammed down the phone our future would have remained grey, but not unbearable. We'd never have watched Cat Guthrie die, never heard Dr Toylar laugh or seen Cort Neilsen smile. We'd never have entered Stethno's House . . . the House of the Gorgon.

'Oh, very well.' I still hesitated and Lady L. gave a contemptuous snort. 'If you refuse to give me your address and waste time and money that is your business. You will just have to come to us. We reside near Regent's Park and had hoped to save you a taxi fare or a long, tedious journey by public transport. The telephone exchange shows that you live out in the suburbs; Harrow and Wealdstone.' She made the area sound like Sodom and Gomorrah. 'I'd intended sending a car to fetch you, and my chauffeur would have delivered proof of our good faith; fifty pounds in cash.

'That's better, Mr Easter.' Fifty quid is not much, but I'd decided to play ball and she paused to jot down the information. 'Number 88A, Ernest Bevin Avenue; what a revolting street name!'

A fair comment, though the sneer did not become a titled lady. Peggy and I would much rather have been housed near Regent's Park, but Bevin was all we'd got. Nor would we have Ernie for long if the landlord's eviction order went through.

'The car will be there to collect you in exactly . . .' She paused a second time to calculate the schedule and I knew that her chauffeur would have to observe that schedule or be out of a job. '. . . in exactly forty-five minutes, Mr Easter, so please see that you and Mrs Tey are ready.' There was a click and the line went dead.

Lady Lesley Wellington Booth was a woman of her word, and a martinet who demanded efficient service and made sure she got it. In spite of the rush-hour traffic there was a sharp rap on our door at the precise moment she'd stated.

That did not surprise me in the least, but her chauffeur certainly did. Madam's arrogant, domineering tone had made me think of country life in pre-war times. Those happy days for the upper classes when a pound sterling was worth five U.S. dollars and the gentry could lord it over their inferiors; retainers, lackeys and elderly, forelock-pulling rustics, and I'd expected that some such forelock-puller would call to collect us. An ex-gillie or gamekeeper relegated from copse to steering wheel by infirmity or age, but I was wrong.

The man on the doorstep was young. He was in fine physical fettle and I'd seen him before. Not in the flesh, thank God, but in a hundred photographs depicting the *Herrenvolk* at their zenith. Though his high-fronted cap lacked a death's-head badge and there were no S.S. flashes on his black uniform, he would have gladdened Himmler's heart. Tall, blond, upright; every inch an Aryan.

'William Easter and Margaret Tey?' His accent was broad

cockney, but the question was delivered and my answer acknowledged in the best Teutonic style. When I nodded, his boots crashed together and he bowed like Prussian officers are supposed to bow. A flamboyant gesture which might have had unfortunate results. The peak of his cap missed my nose by half-an-inch and could easily have broken it.

'Then will you please accompany me immediately.' He spoke as though we were a brace of racial undesirables being carted off to Auschwitz, and frowned when I hesitated. 'Immediately, Mr Easter. Time is important.'

'We're coming in a moment, but there is a small transaction to be settled first . . .' I had been about to say *Herr Sturmführer*, but checked myself. There's no point in making enemies and a bulge in his well-pressed jacket suggested that Superman was wearing a shoulder holster. 'Your mistress did mention a token of good faith.'

'Perfectly correct, sir, and here is that token.' He bowed again, though less exuberantly, and held out a thin wad of fivers. 'Fifty pounds was the agreed sum. You have no need to examine them.' I was checking the notes to see that they weren't forgeries with identical serial numbers and his eyes hardened – bright, china-blue eyes which several prominent murderers are supposed to have possessed.

'My master and my mistress are honourable people. They are also impatient people and you would be foolish to keep them waiting.' He patted the concealed holster and nodded at the door. 'Please do what I say, Mr Easter. The car is outside.'

The car was outside. Peggy and I could see it through the doorway and we followed our driver obediently. We hurried out of the flat, and not just because of his gun or the hope of reward. Curiosity can be as strong as fear or greed and we were both boiling with curiosity.

We had expected to receive an aged, domestic retainer and had been greeted by a heel-clicking, cockney Horst Wessel. We'd imagined that Lady Lesley might run to a Daimler or even a Rolls, but the vehicle parked by the kerb was far more spectacular. A world-war Humber staff car with camouflage paint preserved and battle scars still in evidence. The dents of missiles which had bounced off the bodywork without reaching a human target. The glass windows and metal panels were bulletproof, and after we'd climbed into the rear compartment the door crashed behind us like the slab of a vault.

A collector's piece, if you like such things, which I don't. The relic was heavily sprung and the seats were unpadded. A most uncomfortable form of transport, though there was nothing wrong with it mechanically. The engine had been supercharged and the Nazi impersonator might have won a few laurel wreaths as a racing driver.

Night had started to fall, the rush hour was over, and he wove through the thinning traffic as though dashing to rescue *der Führer* from the Berlin bunker. Peggy and I were thrown forward whenever he failed to beat a traffic signal and jammed on the brakes. We were jerked back as soon as the lights turned green and he accelerated. We were flung sideways at every bend and roundabout. When he reached an Inner London motorway and really let the vehicle have her head we gritted our teeth.

Not a journey for contemplation or quiet discussion, but we'd done a bit of talking before Horst Wessel and his horrible conveyance arrived and asked ourselves some questions. What exactly did Lady Lesley want with us? Why should our acquaintance with a taste for gin have named me as a beneficiary?

There was no doubt who that acquaintance was, or rather had been. The Right Reverend Gerald Hurst-Hutchins, D.D., Lord Bishop of the Anglican Communion. Former president of the independent, sovereign Republic of Leonia, which is a fever-ridden dump on the West Coast of Africa.

Nominally president, I should say. Bishop Gerry had ruled as an absolute dictator till his bone-headed subjects finally rumbled him and he was returned to his maker in a sad state of disrepair. I'd actually seen pictures of children stoning his huge battered body while it swung from the lamp-post.

There was no doubt that pal Gerry was dead, and I was equally certain that he'd died rich. The bishop had milked Leonia's economy dry during his term of office and the loot would be safely stored away in a Swiss bank account. The Wellington Booth woman had spoken the truth on that score, but there was one point which I couldn't understand. Why should Hurst-Hutchins have mentioned me in his will? On our last meeting I'd tried to strangle the bastard.

But enlightenment should soon be forthcoming. The Humber had lurched to a halt before a large Georgian terraced house, and the chauffeur had honked his horn and climbed out. The house door opened immediately and another Third Reich character appeared and motioned us up the short flight of steps leading to the entrance hall. A female domestic, and a most impressive female. Six feet tall, and buxom as Brünnhilde, straight as a ramrod and smart as a drill sergeant. Her khaki uniform was so stiff with starch that I heard it creak as she closed the door behind us. Another example of the *Übermensch* – a real credit to *Das Bund Deutscher Mädel.*

'Her Ladyship says you are to wait here till the Master is able to receive you.' Unlike the chauffeur she had a guttural foreign accent, which might have been German, and though her English vocabulary was fluent there was something odd about the way she emphasized the term *master*. 'The Master is having trouble adjusting his leg, but there is always the chair, so make yourselves comfortable.'

'Thank you.' Though she had nodded at a grim, horsehair sofa, I couldn't see any chair. Apart from a bookcase, a hat-and-coat rack and a table supporting a telephone, the sofa was the only piece of furniture in the equally grim hall, a bare, Spartan room with a colour scheme that matched the maid's uniform. A brown carpet covered the floor, the walls were panelled a dark-brown oak, russet curtains draped the windows. The table was mahogany, parchment-shaded lamps glinted on the brown leather bindings in the bookshelves, and the doors and skirting-boards had been varnished chocolate brown. The atmosphere was as cheerful as a country Welsh chapel during an epidemic of foot-and-mouth disease, and menacing too. Both Peg and I had a feeling that we might need to get out quickly, so we declined Brünnhilde's offer of the sofa and said we preferred to stand.

'Then stand if you wish.' She shrugged a pair of muscular shoulders. 'That is your affair, but you may have to wait some time for the Master.' She marched away through an open door and my forebodings increased.

The Master! It hadn't sounded as though she was referring to a mere employer or the master of the house. The title had been pronounced with a mixture of awe and admiration as if a much bigger pot was involved.

Much, much bigger, and I wasn't thinking about Gentle Jesus, meek and mild. An ungentlemanly character with a colour fixation worried me, and I stared around the gloomy room and considered his associations with colour. Born in *Braunau* – founded the *Brown* Shirts – held meetings at the *Brown* House – married Eva *Braun*.

'It's not possible, Bill.' Peggy shared my suspicions, and she whispered anxiously, moist breath spraying my ear-hole. 'They committed suicide, darling. She took poison and he blew out his brains. All the witnesses – all the historians agreed that he died.'

'Of course he's dead.' I tried to reassure myself as well as Peggy, but doubt was rising. Witnesses lie – experts can be proved wrong. Was there a chance that the experts had been wrong in this instance? A thousand to one chance, but outsiders occasionally win races and miracles do occur. The miracle worker we had in mind made our flesh crawl.

The Master – the chair! Brünnhilde had meant a wheelchair and who would be in it? A man – an old man? Very old, almost ninety years old, but a cunning man who might have fooled them all and got away. A man who had once ravaged the world . . . who had spread terror and misery and claimed more victims than the plague.

Quite impossible. Too sinister for serious consideration, but I was glad of Peg's company because the truth was about to be revealed. Whoever the Master might be, he had fixed his troublesome leg and the wheelchair was not required. We heard a steel foot thumping floorboards. We saw a steel hand appear through the open door. We gasped with relief as a face smiled at us beneath a steel-capped skull.

Not the face of Adolf Hitler, though almost as familiar, and I cursed my memory and the cartoonists and hack writers who think it clever to invent nicknames for public figures: Winnie and Tricky Dicky, Supermac and Uncle Joe. Wellington Booth had conveyed nothing to me, but our host's slang appellations did: Wellie Boy – Jimmy Jackboot – the Crazy Colonel.

'Kind of you to come – most civil.' Colonel Sir James Harcourt Wellington Booth was dressed in mufti, but his medal ribbons were proudly displayed on a brown Harris Tweed jacket, and he had reason to be proud of them. He sported a D.S.O. and an M.C., and a dozen other decorations I couldn't recognize. Jimmy Jackboot had been a national hero before he went potty.

And not as potty as all that. His British Loyalists, a force of volunteers recruited to run the country in the event of crippling strikes, student anarchy and general unrest, was a sound scheme. I might have signed on myself if I'd been in England at the time. The perks were good and I've no time for work-shy layabouts and screeching students. I admire courage and old Booth certainly possessed that quality. He'd sacrificed the top of his skull while covering the retreat to Dunkirk, been deprived of his right hand at El Alamein, and a bomb had blown off his left leg when he was recuperating from that last injury in a base hospital.

A brave man. Perhaps a bit on the short side for a soldier, but courage has no connection with height and a game bantam cock will knock hell out of any hulking barnyard rooster.

The trouble was that the little colonel was too game, too fanatical and too much influenced by his former enemies, the Nazis. The British Loyalists soon blossomed into a miniature army, drilled, armed, dedicated and raring to go.

When they did have their go, a gang of Maoist malcontents from the London School of Economics reaped the whirlwind, and the wind blew violently. Twelve were admitted to hospital suffering from shock and minor injuries, eight were maimed for life, three died.

An excellent score, but as usual the authorities took fright and sided with the malcontents. The Loyalists were declared an illegal organization. Jimmy Jackboot lost his command.

'Yes, exceedingly kind and I'm delighted to meet you, Mr and

Mrs Easter.' Though he must have known we weren't married, courtesy cost nothing and the colonel beamed at Peg and held out his metal hand to shake mine. An agonizing experience; rather like the cliché of having your fingers crushed in a vice, but it wasn't pain that made me wince. Shock did.

Two people had followed Booth into the hall. The first was a woman and quite a pretty woman, if you didn't look at her closely, and I hardly gave her a glance.

I looked at the man behind her . . . the ghost of a man.

2

'Thank you, Lady Lesley. You are kindness personified.' The Booths had led us out of the gloomy hall into a sitting-room which was almost as gloomy, and the man who should have been dead watched our hostess open a drink cupboard.

'And do calm yourself, my dear, I am not a ghost and I was not suspended on that street lamp.' Bishop Gerald Hurst-Hutchins, ex-president of Leonia, smirked at Peggy, who was still gaping with surprise. 'An unfortunate fellow who acted as my understudy reaped the mob's fury and I escaped across the border into Galando. I am very much alive, though a mere shadow of my former self.'

That was certainly true. Whenever I'd seen Hurst-Hutchins in the past he'd been dressed in full canonicals and radiated self-assurance and health, if anyone who weighs twenty stone can be described as healthy. Now, his face was the same colour as the shabby grey suit which hung around him in folds. His body had shrunk, though there was still too much flesh on him, and he was a bag of nerves. His hand shook as he took a glass of gin and lemonade from Lady Lesley, and I saw a little tic trembling beneath each of his bloodshot eyes. The Lord Bishop resembled a vicious caricature of the Tichborne claimant: Thomas Castro – *Bullocky* Orton.

'My sufferings have been considerable, Peggy, and without the charity of our hosts and other good friends I would be in sore straits.' Lady Lesley had provided him with a straw and he sucked at the gin fizz to toast the Wellington Booths. 'But *nil desperandum* is a sound motto and I am blessed with a sanguine nature. All is not lost, because my vice-president, Mr Nathaniel Swarmi, is in London, and he and the embassy staff have remained loyal to my cause. I also know that I can rely on your loyalty, Bill.'

It was my turn to receive a toast and a smirk, but I didn't smile back. I'd worked for the bishop when he had power and money, and on each occasion he'd sold me down the river. I wasn't going to help a pauper on the run, but I might inform the new Leonian government that Gerry was alive and kicking and ask what price they'd pay for his head.

'Stop those silly notions and have a drink, Mr Easter.' Lady Lesley had read my thoughts like a book. 'We know that you are a deceitful and mercenary man, but we did not imagine you were a fool.' She stalked past me on her way back to the booze cupboard and I saw that I was right about her face. A pretty woman at first glance, but she wouldn't stand up to close inspection. The lips were too thin, and the sharp, intelligent eyes were too hard and too callous for beauty. Though she was much younger than the crippled colonel, I felt fairly sure that she'd been the brains behind his disbanded army. I was completely sure that the remnants of that army would have me for breakfast if I did any Hurst-Hutchins selling.

'The bishop told us that Mrs Tey takes sherry and you are addicted to Scotch, Mr Easter.' The cow stressed our unmarried state and was equally insolent about my drinking habits. I do enjoy a drop of whisky, but I've never been a lush.

'Good.' She motioned us to chairs and poured out the drinks. Peg got a generous schooner of Amontillado, but my ration was a mean public-house single measure drowned with water. 'And now that you're both comfortable we shall state our proposition.' She sounded like a Victorian housewife offering employment to a couple of slaveys. 'I shall begin by saying that, though Bishop Hurst-Hutchins is out of office at the moment, he is definitely not down and out. If his suspicions are correct, there will be ample rewards for all of us.' She nodded at Hurst-Hutchins. 'Perhaps you would outline the situation, Gerald.'

'As you wish, dear lady.' He proceeded to do so in much harrowing detail, though he didn't harrow me. The story was a squalid admission of cowardice, deception and inefficiency told in four episodes.

Gerry had gradually realized that he'd swindled the Leonians too flagrantly and that revolt was in the offing. His craven fear had made him hire a double; an oversized out-of-work actor to impersonate him at public functions and be the target for any bombs or bullets. He had completely miscalculated the extent of public unrest and the power of the rebels; the revolution had broken out far sooner than his secret police had anticipated, and the president had fled the country leaving his double to take the rap. That ruse had saved him, but he'd also had to leave his Swiss bank-account numbers behind. He had crossed the frontier incognito and with only a few hundred dollars in his pocket, just enough money to bribe a venal sea captain to ship him back to England, registered as a second steward.

Very sad and tragic in Hurst-Hutchins's own view, but he had friends and, as Lady Lesley had stated, all was not lost. The rebel leaders were as corrupt as the bishop and even more inept. Leonia's economy was reeling, the prisons crammed, and the firing squads running short of ammunition. Gerry might be welcomed back if he returned to Leonia with ample forces at his disposal.

'A force which is ready and waiting.' Colonel Booth broke in to dismiss the sad past and outline a rosy future. 'We can assemble a thousand top-line volunteers, who are ready to invade Leonia at a moment's notice. And when I say *top-line* I mean it. Ex-Desert Rats, ex-commandos, ex-navy wallahs and ex-R.A.F. types.

'Not only British volunteers either. Foreigners of the right calibre are included.' Jimmy Jackboot produced a notebook from his breast pocket and listed a few more superannuated heroes: American Marines, nostalgic for Korea; Luftwaffe pilots reminiscing over Warsaw and Rotterdam; fugitives from the Algerian O.A.S.

'Middle-aged on the whole, but fit as fiddles, Mr Easter. My adjutant, Major Bragshaw, won two Cambridge blues for running and rugger, Peter Cutler the R.S.M. was a welter-weight, Golden

Gloves champion, and I don't need to tell you that my missus is an Olympic equestrienne.' He didn't have to tell me. Lady Lesley had almost flogged a horse to death while earning her honours, but I bowed politely to keep them happy. A crazy, bent trio, but they'd begun to interest me.

'More important than physical fitness, my chaps are all trained fighting men with specialized civilian skills – engineers and admin. officers, medicos and mechanics, transport and communication experts.

'Men who know how to handle men . . . men who can run a country. Could anyone stop such men, Mr Easter?'

'Many people could, sir.' I spoke sceptically, because I'm sceptical by nature, but my interest was increasing. Booth's long-in-the-tooth warriors had been disbanded and they were bored and frustrated and thirsting for action. If the band of hope reached Leonia they might be able to topple the new regime and restore Hurst-Hutchins to power. There were some snags, however, and I mentioned one of them. 'What about the United Nations?'

'No problem, Bill. None of the major powers wish to become involved in Leonian affairs and the rebel government is not yet recognized by the U.S. Since my sad demise, Nathaniel Swarmi has been regarded as the titular head of state, and Nathaniel will do exactly what I tell him.' The bishop emphasized his answers with a girlish giggle. 'The sole difficulty is to purchase equipment for the invasion, and transport our forces to Leonia. We need ships and aircraft, arms, ammunition and general supplies.' He ticked off the needs on his pudgy fingers. 'Finance is required, in fact, and I can hardly approach a bank without revealing my presence in London and running the risk of assassination.

'A frustrating problem, but it must be solved and that is why we have asked you here.' He raised the straw to his lips and pulled at the gin fizz. 'I have a feeling that, with God's grace, you and Peggy will provide all the money we want.'

'Then you must be out of your mind.' Peg snorted as scornfully as Lady Lesley had done on the telephone. 'Apart from that fifty quid we got from the chauffeur Bill and I are penniless.'

'At the moment, my dear, but one must think ahead.' The straw made an unpleasant squelching sound as Hurst-Hutchins sucked the dregs from his glass. 'Like Colonel Booth's veterans, you are both persons with specialized skills and I am a dreamer. If my present dream is correct and your skills reap fruit, the problem is solved.' He lowered the glass and smiled at Peggy.

'We will soon be rolling in filthy lucre and this is all you have to do.' The bishop was still staring at Peg, but he'd stopped smiling. The sagging face hardened like lava turning to rock and it made me think of a Greek mask representing determination.

'You and Bill are going to locate, inspect and recover the Calamai treasure.'

Locate the Calamai treasure! I've met a lot of idiots as well as villains in my time and listened to their idiotic statements. But H.-H.'s statement was the most idiotic of the lot and it seemed clear that his tribulations in Leonia had caused serious brain damage.

Locate indeed! Everybody with a smattering of education knows where the Calamai treasure can be located. A hundred people gape at the exhibits daily, though they don't touch them. The collection is lodged in the Danemere Museum, South Kensington, and the museum is as secure as the Bank of England. In case you haven't got much education, I'll put you in the picture.

Lord Walter Danemere, the founder of the feast, was a successful eighteenth-century slave trader who developed a conscience during his declining years and bequeathed his house and fortune in trust to the nation. The will, which was made on Danemere's death bed, stated that all liquid assets should be prudently invested and the profits used to purchase works of art and historical interest. Instructions the senile do-gooder wouldn't have regretted, because his original trustees were shrewd knowledgeable men, as were their successors. Lord Walter's bequest had become as swollen as one of his slave schooners. If the exhibits on view in the museum were for sale, it would take an oil-swollen Arab sheikh to buy them.

Only on view, and definitely not for sale. None of the more valuable pieces could be closely examined without the curator's personal authorization and that authority was difficult to obtain and impossible to defy. Though the building was old it had many modern innovations to deter the reckless. Electric beams which activated burglar alarms and slammed doors. Plate-glass panels and magnetically operated shutters that shot down like guillotine blades if you tried to break the glass. I once knew a chap who did make such an attempt and it was a rash act. Like Colonel Sir James Wellington Booth he lost his right hand.

Locate, inspect and recover! What balderdash! The Danemere Museum was not my cup of tea and I told Hurst-Hutchins so in no uncertain terms. If he hoped to steal the Calamai treasure he could count Peg and I out and find himself a couple of masochists.

'Steal, Bill?' My refusal raised a mournful sigh. 'What do you take me for? I am not a thief, and theft has never crossed my mind.'

True enough. The bishop wasn't a thief, because he hadn't got the courage to steal anything. He was a manipulator who hired others to do his dirty work, and I told him that too.

'Manipulator? I rather approve of that description, Billy Boy.' Old Booth had discarded formality and his eyes twinkled. We were members of the gang, but I was sure the twinkle would have faded if I'd been equally hearty and called him Wellie or Jimmy Jackboot. 'The bishop, my wife and myself are manipulators and proud of the title. We do employ people; the best people, and in the circumstances you are the very best.

'That is why you're on our payroll, and I'm delighted to introduce you to another most valued employee.' The door had opened bang on cue and he beamed at the woman who came into the room – a dowdy, mousy, spinster type who looked as though she spent her leisure hours knitting socks for relatives' children.

'Prompt as usual, Jan, and nice to see you as usual.' Booth's metal pincers tapped her arm and my opinion of the visitor appeared to be correct. She carried a string bag which bulged with articles of clothing. 'You've met Bishop Hurst-Hutchins, of course, and here are Mr and Mrs Easter, the two rookies I told you about; Bill and Peg to us now.' The presumptuous little bastard grinned presumptuously.

'This is Miss Janet Sweeting, a former commander in the Auxiliary Territorials and my valued assistant at Department Zero.' He motioned us to shake hands with the woman and I remembered hearing about the Zero business. War wounds had not ended the bantam cock's military career. Though field service was prohibited, he'd been given a desk job with army intelligence and performed his duties energetically for several years. Far too energetically; Zero was disbanded after the ambassador of a friendly power discovered a microphone under his bed. The fact that he had a mistress on top of the bed did not mitigate the circumstances and Booth got his marching orders.

'Aunty Jan, as we all called her, was quite indispensable to the department and loved by the entire section.'

'You are too kind, Colonel, and I hope that my current efforts meet with your approval.' Aunty rummaged in her bag and produced an envelope hidden between a half-finished jumper and a pair of gloves. 'Bishop Hurst-Hutchins has promised that his embassy staff will supply us with blank Leonian passports and the other necessary documents. Seals, photographs and so forth can easily be added. There should be no trouble on that score.

'But this article did present some problems, because the balance has to be exact. Enthusiastic and flattering, but not too flattering. Not fulsome enough to arouse suspicion.' She drew a sheet of paper from the envelope. 'I also had difficulty in obtaining the correct typeface at such short notice; an eight-point Albion, which is rarely used today.'

'I don't imagine our chappie knows much about typefaces. It's the composition that counts, Jan, so let's have a squint at what you've written.' Booth donned a pair of thick tortoiseshell glasses for the squint and beamed approvingly when he came to the end of Miss Sweeting's production.

'Not bad, Aunty. Deuced good in my view. "A play to catch the conscience of the king".' He misquoted pompously and inaccurately and handed the exhibit to his wife. 'Don't you agree, Lesley?'

The Olympic medallist did agree with equal enthusiasm and so did Hurst-Hutchins. The bishop positively chortled after examining the document and asking for my opinion. 'What do you say, Bill?'

What the hell could I say? The paper appeared to be a backdated clipping from the *West-African Eagle*, Leonia's official journal before the revolution. A propagandist rag controlled by Hurst-Hutchins, edited by his toadies, and censored by his secret police in case those toadies stepped out of line. The last copies I'd seen were filled with warnings to would-be traitors and promises of future prosperity; promises which would never be fulfilled. The Lord Bishop had pocketed the funds.

The *Eagle* had also devoted space to sport and gossip, but I hadn't noticed any literary section, which was understandable. The average Leonian is illiterate, and Miss Sweeting's contribution seemed out of keeping. The review of a book entitled *Renaissance Goldsmiths* by someone called Samuel Swayle, M.A. (Cantab.). A bloody favourable review, as Aunty intended, and if I was Sam Swayle I'd have jumped for joy.

'The work of a truly professional scholar . . . A fountain of knowledge and information which will enthral every reader . . . A delightful piece of research combining education, entertainment and romance . . . As profound as Einstein, as compulsive as Agatha Christie . . .'

Enthusiastic and flattering! The extracts I've quoted were just a few verses from the song of praise and there was only one adverse comment. 'Mr Swayle's chapter on Guido Andrea Calamai appears sketchy and slightly inaccurate; the sole flaw in this otherwise admirable book.'

Yes, a bloody nice notice, though I couldn't understand why Aunty Jan had written it or forged a copy of the *Eagle*. I didn't understand a thing till I reached the end of the review and a line of type seemed to leap from the paper and slam me in the eyes.

The reviewer claimed to be a history professor at the University of Constitution, which is Leonia's major seat of learning. The professor's name was William Easter.

3

'How pleasant it is to talk to kindred spirits.' Mr Samuel Swayle, curator of the Danemere Museum and author of *Renaissance Gold-*

smiths, beamed at Peggy and myself and he had reason to beam. Aunty Jan Sweeting had invented a crafty trap and baited it well. Mr Swayle was delighted by our visit.

A man spends years writing a dud book, which he considers a masterpiece, and he waits eagerly for publication date and the glowing reviews to follow. But what does the poor boob get? Abuse, contempt, rejection, and depressing news when he asks his publisher for the sales figures.

Most disappointing, but Sam Swayle had received belated consolation. A rave notice in a widely distributed African newspaper and penned by a fellow savant, William Easter, Professor of History at the University of Constitution. The professor happened to be holidaying in England and he had posted the author a copy of his review and an explanatory letter requesting that they might meet and discuss the opus together.

Better still, Professor Easter had asked if he could bring along a colleague. Mrs Margaret Tey, chief adviser to Leonia's Minister of Education, was equally enthusiastic about the *Goldsmiths* and hoped to persuade her minister to make the book compulsory reading in every Leonian college and high school.

Mrs Tey had an even more attractive proposition in mind. Black Africa was beginning its own Renaissance and yearning for culture. If Mr Swayle was agreeable, the minister might sponsor a lecture tour, a slap-up international affair which would start at Constitution, Leonia's capital, and ignite the torch of learning across an entire continent.

'Yes, a real pleasure, and do have some more sherry.' Swayle was not merely agreeable to undertake Peg's tour. He could already hear applause ringing around the lecture halls. His smile widened when he picked up the bottle, and his hand was quite steady as he refilled the glasses, though he'd recently suffered a severe shock.

Three hours before our arrival, a bomb had been detonated in the museum and the place still reeked of gelignite and burnt flesh. Little damage was done, but the event proved that I was right in telling Hurst-Hutchins that the Danemere treasures were well guarded.

The bomb-toter, a lout appropriately named O'Hooligan, had

been rumbled immediately because he didn't know that the building was fitted with an ingenious system which could detect the smell of explosives. A warning bell rang as soon as O'Hooligan entered the portico and two security officers watched his progress on a television scanner. Patient, intelligent men with a taste for survival and no love of heroics. Why shoot it out with a terrorist if there's a button handy? They pressed the button after their suspect reached a deserted corridor leading to the Egyptian hall and he was left to his own devices. Magnetically operated doors sealed the area and, when the bomb went off, the sole sufferers were its owner and Bast, the Cat God. Bast's statue lost a paw and was liberally spattered with O'Hooligan's mortal remains.

A trivial incident, though it caused Peggy and I some anxiety because the museum was closed to the public and swarming with police. Before gaining admission to the curator's office, we'd been questioned and searched, though to no avail. I'm a good con man providing I don't have to assume a completely false identity or act under another name. Professor Christmas or Professor Lent might have been unconvincing, but Professor Easter was an easy role and Miss Sweeting was a skilful forger. The rozzers swallowed my story hook, line and sinker, and never suspected that our well-worn Leonian passports, credit cards and driving licences were fresh from the press, and the stamps registering our arrival at London Airport slightly inaccurate. Nor did they examine the felt-tipped pen in my pocket, and God help us if they had. The Booths and Hurst-Hutchins were reticent employers. They'd told us what to do, but not why it should be done. I hadn't a clue what they were up to, but I did know one thing. That little pen could send us to prison for a long, long time. I could almost feel it pulsing against my skin.

But our troubles seemed to be past, because Sam Swayle was far less suspicious than the police. He fawned on us and complimented me on my academic attainments; as well he might. A chap called Easter had received a London double-first at about the same time I was booted out of Oxford and Swayle naturally believed we were one and the same. Nor did he question Peggy's qualifications. Her letter of introduction from the minister was impeccable and you don't look a gift horse in the mouth. Not a horse that's going to double your sales and bring you fame and fortune.

'Cheers to you both.' Swayle's own mouth had badly fitting dentures and they clicked while he toasted us. 'Also thank you both, because you are the first scholars to appreciate my work.' He smiled at a copy of *Renaissance Goldsmiths* displayed on his desk with Aunty Jan's bogus review beside it.

'When I think of the sneers and insults I received . . . when I consider Tom Moscow's deliberate attempts to hamper and frustrate me, I sometimes forget my Christian upbringing.' The smile faded and he frowned at a row of oil paintings lining the study walls, portraits of the museum's former curators and trustees, starting with Lord Danemere who had set the ball rolling in 1789. The repentant slaver looked as benevolent as Mr Pickwick, but one couldn't say the same about Swayle's predecessor. Sir Thomas Moscow resembled a hanging judge and the artist hadn't attempted to soften his expression. Moscow's eyes and his grim, granite features made me think of a passage from Shelley. 'I met murder on the way, he had a face like Castlereagh.'

'Old Tom Moscow was an expert, I suppose, but difficult to work with. Difficult and intolerant and, as they say, the best minds are the first to crack. Present company excepted, of course.'

Swayle apologized for the social bloomer, but his eyes remained fixed on Moscow's portrait. 'Extremely difficult, though one must be charitable, because the poor man probably couldn't help himself. There was, and still is madness in the Moscow family. Tom's father also committed suicide and his unfortunate daughter is a permanent resident at Normanton Towers, Dr Toylar's mental institution not far from Guildford.

'All very, very sad.' Swayle sighed, but more in self-pity than sympathy for the ill-fated Moscows, and I didn't blame him. He'd been Sir Thomas's assistant for six years and it must have been a miserable span. If the picture was any guide to character I'd rather have worked for Beelzebub.

'Tom was a lineal descendent of Lord Danemere, of course, which might explain his obsession with security, but to actually believe that the . . .' The curator broke off, obviously feeling that he was talking out of school, but there was no need for him to finish the sentence. We'd been briefed about the late, unlamented Moscow and knew what his belief was. The man had gone potty and started to consider that the museum was his personal property. He'd even consulted lawyers in the hope of contesting Danemere's bequest to the nation and grabbing it himself.

'An obsession with security,' I said, sipping at the sherry, which was sweet and oily and quite repulsive. 'Today's event suggests that his precautions were justified.'

'Possibly, Professor, and Tom persuaded the trustees to give him *carte blanche*; or rather he bullied them into doing so.' Swayle was still staring at the painting like a rabbit hypnotized by a stoat. 'But the money we spent on those anti-burglar devices could have purchased a Rembrandt, and when one considers the fur collection . . .' He finally pulled his eyes away from the likeness of his persecutor and grimaced.

'Some of the items are interesting, of course. We've got a set of Queen Victoria's sea-otter tippets, an ermine cloak which belonged to Catherine the Great, and an astrakhan cap Napoleon wore during one of his victories. The battle was Marengo in my opinion, though some historians disagree and favour Austerlitz.

'Interesting and perishable, but they'd be perfectly safe in moth-proof cases, and Tom installed an electric refrigerating plant. He had a bee in his bonnet about preservation which was almost as strong as the security bug.' Swayle's false teeth clicked indignantly.

'Wanton, insane extravagance, but poor Tom *was* insane. Mania and superstitious fear of Calamai's curse destroyed him and that's why he died in such a horrible manner.' The curator shook his head and turned to Peggy. 'Quite mad, Mrs Tey, and you'll hardly believe this, Madam. When I started my chapter on Guido Calamai, Tom refused to let me handle the collection. Nobody except himself was allowed to handle them and that is true today. Before Tom recommended me as his successor, I had to swear an oath that I would continue the prohibition.'

'An oath which I'm sure you will break in the interest of learning, Mr Swale.' Peggy stroked the book as though it was a kitten and frowned at my review. 'What an admirable thesis this is,

Curator. What a shame that Professor Easter is sceptical regarding your views on the Calamai dinner service.

'Mistakenly sceptical in my opinion, but I'm afraid our minister will require proof that the professor is wrong.' Peg is an excellent actress and a born bully. Her iron-fist, velvet-glove attitude was as professional as *Renaissance Goldsmiths* was an amateurish flop.

I'd read the damn book. I'd read it three times, paying particular attention to the Calamai section, and though I'm not a metallurgist or a historian, I do know about gold and goldsmiths. I'm not sure why, but gold has always fascinated me. Maybe it's the gloss or the weight or the untarnishable lustre of the stuff. Maybe legend and folklore play a part. The Apples of Hesperides, the yellow crock at a rainbow's end, El Dorado; the kingdom of the great, golden man.

Perhaps pure greed is responsible, but I do know about gold and I can recognize a piece of bungling plagiarism on the subject. Sam Swayle, M.A. hadn't done his homework. He'd twisted facts and cribbed from other authors. The reviewers had been quite right to take him to task.

'You believe that our Calamai exhibits are not entirely genuine, Professor Easter? You want to examine them personally?' I'd stated my doubts in the covering letter and Swayle's face was a study of conflicting emotions. Loyalty to a dead employer he had hated. Anxiety that the Leonian government would turn him down. There was also a third emotion which I didn't recognize for a while. 'You consider that Calamai was too ill to complete his commission and the duchess employed a minor craftsman to finish the set?'

'Believe and consider are strong words, Curator. I merely suspect since all Calamai's career is suspicious.' I lit a cigarette and proceeded to outline that career, partly to refresh my memory and partly to show that I knew the biographical data.

An exciting biography, because Guido Andrea Decimo Calamai was an exciting man. A typical mid-renaissance progeny, devoid of morals but bursting with genius. During his short life, which ended at the age of twenty-seven, he'd amassed a fortune, produced a hundred masterpieces and speared more maidenheads than a Turkish sultan. He'd also swindled a pope and a Venetian banker, killed three men in tavern brawls, and probably murdered ten times that number by poison.

Enviable achievements, but Guido finally met his match and it was a lady without a maidenhead who got him in the end. The maestro contracted gonorrhoea while working on his final commission, and the commissioner was his last patron and last mistress. Maria Fenterelli, the Duchessa di Palento, gave Calamai the clap, and he died cursing her and his own creation: a classical dinner service, now known as the Danemere treasure. I can't remember exactly how the curse was worded, but the threat was pretty grim. The duchess and her dinner service and all its future owners and admirers were condemned to death and damnation.

Words which bore fruit. Maria Fenterelli soon followed Calamai into the grave and several of her descendants experienced untimely deaths. Accidents, assassinations and disease ravaged the family till they sold the treasure to an English *milord* making the Grand Tour. *Milord* got himself a bargain, but he didn't enjoy it for long. On returning to England he started to believe he was a werewolf and acted accordingly. Half-a-dozen women were savaged before he was caught red-handed and red-toothed and locked away in a padded cell. His son heeded the warning and presented Calamai's *objet d'art* to the Danemere.

There'd been no more sad occurrences since then, not unless you count Moscow's suicide, and Jackboot Booth had ridiculed any supernatural intervention on that score with customary bluntness. 'Bad blood . . . tainted stock . . . bats in the belfry,' was the fighting cock's verdict.

'I don't have to remind you that Guido Calamai was generations ahead of his time and discovered that no set of fingerprints are identical, Mr Swayle.' Professor Easter opened his briefcase with a flourish. 'For that reason he made a metal caste of his left index finger and hallmarked all his works with its stamp.' I held out an enlarged photograph of the print. 'Does the Danemere dinner service bear that stamp, sir? Every item of the service?'

'They are certainly hallmarked in such a way, Professor, but I must admit that I have never – never – studied the prints closely.' Swayle had a slight stammer which was becoming more pronounced. 'However, Tom Moscow gave me his word that they are identical to other authenticated Calamai pieces like the Vatican mirror, the statuette of Mars in the Louvre, the Heidelberg satyr.'

'You accepted the word of a man you have described as a maniac, Mr Swayle?' I adopted the tone some genuine professor might have used to humiliate a dim-witted student. 'Not good enough, I'm afraid. If Mrs Tey is to recommend your book to our minister, those marks must be checked thoroughly.'

'Thoroughly and *immediately*, Curator, because there is no time to waste, and I am returning to Leonia at the end of the week.' Peg supported me with equal firmness. 'Syllabuses for the academic year must be prepared. An itinerary of your lecture tour must be planned.'

'You mean that you wish to inspect the collection today . . . at this very moment?' We both nodded emphatically, but the poor booby still hesitated and I realized why. Not from loyalty to a defunct predecessor, and not because he suspected we might be thieves or confidence tricksters. Cowardice was responsible for his reluctance.

We knew that Sir Thomas Moscow was a gullible, superstitious man, and Swayle had stated that he was a lunatic. But Swayle wasn't quite sure, and he didn't want to break his vow and enter the display vault. After Moscow committed suicide the poor booby had started to believe that Guido Calamai's curse might have the power to create agony and death.

How right the poor booby was!

'A disgusting stench.' We'd persuaded Swayle to renounce his oath and pluck up courage and he opened his door and sniffed the air, which still reeked of O'Hooligan's fiery departure. 'However, it's an ill wind, as they say, and I don't suppose any more terrorists will risk following that fellow's example, eh, constable?' He nodded at a policeman on duty outside his sanctum and led the way forward.

Now that the decision had been made, Mr Swayle seemed eager to get the inspection over and his step was almost jaunty as we walked through the halls and corridors dedicated to superstition and the urge to keep up with the Joneses. Winged Assyrian bulls, mummified pharaohs, and African devil masks which looked as though they'd been fashioned by a class of sub-normal juvenile delinquents.

Almost jaunty. The curator still had one anxiety left, and he voiced it after we reached the refrigerated fur collection, and Peg's squeal of enthusiasm halted his progress.

'Isn't that magnificent?' Victoria's tippets were nothing to shout about, and the Marengo / Austerlitz cap resembled a stuffed poodle. But Catherine the Great's ermines were a sight to gladden sore eyes and they certainly gladdened Peggy's. Her pupils glowed with cupidity. 'How I'd love to try them on.'

'So you shall, dear lady.' Swayle beckoned to a janitor and told him to remove the garment from its fridge and hang it over a radiator. 'The cloak should be at a comfortable body heat by the time Professor Easter has completed his findings, Mrs Tey, and very lovely you will look in it.' The curator's sense of duty had gone to the winds and he was no judge of size. The Russian empress was a smallish woman and Peggy's massive shoulders would probably split the seams apart.

'But a sudden thought has just occurred to me, Mrs Tey.' He tried to speak nonchalantly while his assistant opened the case, but I knew he was lying. The thought was not sudden and he'd been considering it for several minutes.

'If we should discover that the dinner service is not entirely the work of Calamai, and a student completed certain items after his death, need that prevent you recommending my book to your minister?' Though he was addressing Peggy, his eyes kept flicking towards mine and I saw the same hypnotized rabbit expression with which he'd looked at Moscow's portrait. I was the stoat now and I had Mr Swayle exactly where I wanted him. He'd carry me up to bed on his back if I gave the word. 'A preface explaining my mistake could easily be added to the book and I would naturally acknowledge Professor Easter's valuable contribution.'

A handsome gesture, and of course the discovery needn't stop Peg's recommendation. Such an admission of error should make the book even more interesting, and the professor would be delighted by a mention in the revised edition. He'd even write the preface himself, if Mr Swayle was willing.

Swayle was not merely willing. He would be honoured and elated and I saw that anxieties had vanished. There was a spring in his stride when we turned away from the furs, and he positively strutted along the road to journey's end. Walter Mitty was already blazing the trail across Africa. I was already starting to believe my pessimism might be groundless. Mechanical precautions, shutters and bars and electric rays, can be rendered useless by human stupidity. We'd conned the Danemere's curator easily, and we might be able to remove its chattels.

I should soon know, because journey's end was in sight, and what an end that was. A small room; less than a tenth the size of the Assyrian and Egyptian halls, but ten times more exciting. Our gold . . . our crock beneath the rainbow. A store house of God-given art . . . a cesspool of exceedingly filthy lucre.

The Calamai dinner service has often been photographed in recent years, but only through the tough, laminated glass which screens it, and from a distance. Sir Thomas Moscow had erected railings to keep spectators well back from the screen, and after Swayle had opened a flap in the railings and motioned us through I realized how inadequate those photographs were. After Swayle twirled the dial of a combination lock and the glass partition slid upwards my spirits rose with it, and I stepped into a treasure trove. An Aladdin's cave, containing two-hundred-and-eighty pieces of solid gold. Imperishable masterpieces, commissioned by a great lady and executed by a major craftsman. After I'd held a magnifying glass over a few of those pieces I damn nearly retched.

There are several biographies of Guido Andrea Calamai and Maria Fenterelli, Duchessa di Palento, and they each agree on the principal facts. The pair became lovers towards the end of their lives and they were both geniuses, though in different fields.

Calamai's talents were devoted to art, lechery and crime, and he also studied herbalism and dabbled in alchemy. An attractive rogue, who sold the philosopher's stone to a gullible count of the Holy Roman Empire, and would probably have sold his own parents if he'd had a buyer for them.

Good luck to Guido on all those scores, because I'm a rogue myself. I appreciate women and beauty and I've always hated my parents. So would you if you'd known them. A father subject to ungovernable rages, and a neurotic, snivelling Mama, constantly accusing me of breaking her heart.

Maria Fenterelli's attainments were political; she was a Machiavellian lass, who crushed three peasant rebellions by guile and fed the leaders to a pack of wolfhounds. Good luck to her also. Dogs must be fed, I suppose.

Estimable characters, but when they joined forces their union bore strange fruit, though the strangeness was only detectable under a lens. The nymphs and shepherds capering around Calamai's soup tureen appeared jolly enough to the naked eye. Venus and Cupid seemed to be enjoying their romp across the dessert plates. The grimmer classical deities – Jupiter and Hercules and Minerva – were suitably noble.

Very nice – very wrong, and very menacing, though not a personal menace. Guido Calamai's curse couldn't harm me, because I didn't find his swan song attractive. My magnifying glass revealed that one of the nymphs and her partner were mottled with plague spots, and the goddess of love shared their symptoms. Cupid's boyish beauty was marred by a harelip and Jupiter's stern features displayed the lion-face thickening attributed to leprosy. Every item I examined depicted an example of disease or deformity and I didn't need Freud to explain why. Guido and Maria were diseased themselves. Sick jesters with a fondness for sick jokes which certainly sickened me.

'The prints, Professor – the hallmarks?' Swayle's impatience interrupted my studies. 'Are they genuine?'

'I'm not sure yet, Curator. Tracings must be compared to the photographs.' I took the felt-tipped pen and a sheet of fine paper from my pocket and leaned towards a goblet which was bracketed to its shelf like the rest of the collection. 'This is one of the little numbers I suspect and it should tell us a great deal. Did Calamai kill the duchess or was someone else involved?'

'The Cyclops goblet . . . the Tainted Chalice, as Moscow called it, Mr Easter?' Swayle was so concerned for my safety that he forgot my title. 'Do please be careful. Tom Moscow was certain he'd removed the venom, but he might have been wrong.'

'Don't worry, Mr Swayle. I've never been afflicted by the death wish.' Though I spoke lightly my nausea increased and I saw what Moscow had meant by *tainted*.

The goblet was a masterpiece worthy of Calamai and his fingerprint had been visible through the lens. But not a vessel any person in the know would drink from. The stem was a gruesome figurine of the blinded Polyphemus and a possible origin of Calamai's curse was evident. Moscow had discovered that Calamai had shared the Borgia's fondness for poison-ring devices. He'd detected and removed the poison, but the means of its transmission remained to show what a humorist the *maestro* was. The rim of the goblet was inlaid with semi-precious stones and one of those stones had a razor-sharp edge and a hole in its centre.

There's many a slip twixt cup and lip, and if your lip had slipped on that cup you might have started to develop a death wish. Death could be your best friend.

'Yes, a couple of tracings should settle the argument, Mr Swayle.' I laid the paper in position, held the little trick pen over it and waited for Peg to sneeze, as she'd been told to do. An admirable sneeze which boomed like a trumpet and drowned the sounds we had to conceal when I pressed a switch on the side of the pen.

The whirl of a tiny electric motor. The gnaw of a drill biting into the Cyclops's blind, metallic eye.

4

'Well done, thou good and faithful servants.' After assuring Mr Swayle that the Calamai hallmarks were all genuine and large numbers of African savants would soon be applauding his lectures and scratching their woolly skulls over his book, Peg and I had returned to the Booth residence and received suitable congratulations. Brief words of praise from the colonel and his lady, and a sanctimonious misquote, this time from Hurst-Hutchins. We'd also been suitably rewarded because Booth was an honourable little chap. He'd handed me another wad of notes as though conferring a degree and said that, if all went well, the two hundred they added up to should be regarded as a small advance payment for further services.

Honourable, but reticent. He refused to state what those services were, or why it had been necessary to deceive old Swayle and mutilate the Cyclops goblet. I only had a vague suspicion, but I was sure about one thing. Our visit had convinced me that the museum's security precautions were impeccable. Disfiguring a drinking vessel was one thing; removing the collection quite another. Unless Swayle could be bribed, which was unlikely because he'd soon rumble us when he failed to hear from Peg's minister, our employers had wasted their money. The Calamai treasure was unstealable and I told them so.

'Bribery has never crossed our minds, Mr Easter, and the bishop assured you that we are neither thieves nor criminals.' Lady Lesley was a keen rider to hounds and her voice cracked like a whip. Not a very vicious crack, however. The trick pen was being passed around and it was her turn to feel its weight, which had increased slightly since Miss Sweeting gave me the thing. A hollow drill concealed in the felt tip had gouged a metal sliver from the cup and the felt was treated with resin to seal the resulting hole. A clever gadget which had fooled old Swayle, but expensive to produce and I couldn't imagine why it had been made. All we'd brought back from the museum was a tiny quantity of gold.

'No details at this juncture, my dear, and there may be no further operations.' Peggy had questioned Booth and he shook his head emphatically. 'I don't want to raise your hopes, but I will explain the general situation.

'My wife and I are gamblers, and on the advice of Bishop Hurst-Hutchins we are contemplating a flutter. A bet on one of the rankest outsiders to be entered in any steeplechase.' He watched Lady Lesley pass the pen to the Sweeting woman. 'Janet will be able to tell us whether our horse appears at the starting gate, but even that should not excite you. There are a lot of fences and water jumps between start and finish.'

'You are still considering theft, Bill?' Aunty Jan had hurried out of the room and Hurst-Hutchins grinned. 'You too, Peggy? What a dishonest couple you are!' He chuckled, but there was no merriment in the noise, and no humour in his grey, sagging face. The nervous tics under his eyes were more pronounced than on our previous visit, and I saw that the Booths had become equally tense. The colonel tapped a table top with his steel fingers, and Lady L. dragged at a cigarette as though it might be her last; a final favour before the firing squad opened up. The conspirators had been pleased by our efforts at the Danemere, but Miss Sweeting was the key witness now. In a few moments they would know whether their horse would run and what the future held for them. Frustration and obscurity, or power and glory? Boredom or battle? A pay chest to send Booth's trigger-happy legions charging off to reconquer Leonia for Hurst-Hutchins?

There might also be a few crumbs for Peggy and myself, and I started to share the common tension, though I hadn't a clue what the project was and enlightenment was not forthcoming. Booth frowned icily when Peg tried to pump him again, so I attempted to control my impatience and relax.

I closed my eyes and listened to a clock ticking away on the mantelshelf. I listened to the faint drone of traffic in the street, and an airliner howling overhead. I listened to the colonel's metal hand drumming against the table, and finally I heard the sounds we were all waiting for. The click of brisk, purposeful footsteps crossing the hall, and the creak of door hinges.

'These are my findings, sir.' Aunty Jan placed a sheet of foolscap on the table and watched Booth's reactions, which created more delay. He polished his glasses before putting them on to check the findings, and he read the data three times before nodding.

'Thank you, Janet. What an indispensable ally you are.' He nodded more vigorously. First to his wife and Hurst-Hutchins, and then to Peggy and myself.

'Tell me, Bill,' he said, and I could almost smell his change of mood. 'If you were a wealthy man – a really wealthy man, how much would you bid for the Danemere's Calamai collection?'

A stupid and simple question. Guido Calamai's masterpieces were not for sale, and if they were I wouldn't have offered a red cent for them. I didn't appreciate the *maestro's* productions and had I been rotten rich I could have thought of far better things to spend my money on. Women, yachts, villas, and a private executive jet to wing me to and from them.

But, though Booth had expressed himself foolishly, I knew what he meant, and I told him that when the treasure was last valued, the figure was around two-and-a-quarter-million pounds.

'At a conservative estimate, Bill Boy, and that valuation was made twelve years ago.' Tension was a thing of the past and the colonel's eyes twinkled gleefully. 'Sterling has depreciated rapidly during those years, so the collection's nominal worth must have risen accordingly. Would you agree that six million was a realistic price at present-day standards?'

I said that six seemed about right and he guffawed and passed Miss Sweeting's notes to Hurst-Hutchins. 'Then you'd be swindling yourself, son. What's your guess, Gerald?'

'I don't need to guess, James. Your tone has given me the answer, and I know the price tag.' The bishop's nervous tic had vanished. There was a hint of colour in his cheeks, and he looked as happy as a kid at a fun-fair. 'My hunch has been proved correct, our horse is ready to run, and the race can now proceed with God's blessing.' His Lordship raised a moist, flabby hand in benediction.

'Colonel Wellington Booth is justified in considering you a spendthrift investor, Bill, but don't be offended. You and Peg were under a disadvantage when you examined the Danemere's exhibits, and I shall tell you what they are really worth.' The hand was lowered on to the shoulder of my jacket and I could almost feel its sweat oozing through the cloth. 'Six million pounds indeed!

'The Danemere's so-called treasure isn't worth six hundred.'

'The Cyclops Goblet has been proved a fake and I am certain that the entire collection is equally phoney.' The bishop had not only regained colour and confidence, he was as elated as Mr Swayle had been when we left him. 'An easy fraud to perpetrate, if you had skill, workshop facilities and privacy.

'All one would need to do is take plaster casts from the original pieces and reproduce them in pinchbeck, an alloy of zinc and copper which resembles gold so closely that only experts can tell the difference.

'Apart from weight, of course, and that's how you and Bill were fooled, my darling.' He leaned forward and gave Peg a slobbery kiss on the cheek. 'Though you touched the exhibits and examined them visibly, you could not judge their weight, because they were held in place by brackets.' The bishop smiled smugly at the Booths. 'It was those brackets which raised my suspicions when I last visited the museum. The Calamai collection is lodged in a vault and protected by complex mechanical devices which would foil the most professional burglar. Why should Tom Moscow have added such simple fastenings which any child could remove with a screwdriver?

'But we know Moscow's motives now. Bill and Peggy have provided the evidence and our technical authority has pronounced judgment.' Miss Sweeting would probably have received a kiss, but she stepped back hurriedly. 'Congratulations, Janet. Thanks to your expertise, my theory is confirmed.'

'Compliments are quite unnecessary, Bishop. Anyone with a smattering of physics can distinguish a copper-zinc alloy from gold.' Aunty Jan spoke sharply. Had old Booth tried to kiss her she might have been pleased, but she shared my dislike of Gerry and his gushing graces. 'Pinchbeck does resemble gold on the surface, but there are three major differences: weight, melting points and durability.

'Whilst gold is virtually indestructible, copper-based alloys dissolve in acid and I used heat and acid to test the specimen Mr and Mrs Easter delivered.' She looked at us as though we were a couple of messenger boys. 'My tests show that the goblet is a pinchbeck forgery, Bishop Hurst-Hutchins, so may we get down to business and prepare our future plans?'

'Not yet, Sweetie.' Aunty's tone had been as acid as her tests, but it didn't dissolve Hurst-Hutchins's good humour and he mocked her name with a smirk. 'You are too impatient, Janet, and I have no future plans at the moment. The past must be considered first.

'Considered and discussed, and discussion is such thirsty work.'

He nodded at the drink cupboard and waited for Lady Lesley to take the hint before repeating himself and continuing.

'Skill, workshop facilities and privacy. The essential requirements for removing two-hundred-and-eighty pieces of precious metal from their storeroom and replacing them with alloy substitutes. Only one man possessed those requirements, and I don't need to tell you who that man was.'

Quite correct; there was no need, but Gerry liked the sound of his own voice so he told us just the same.

'Sir Thomas Moscow; an expert metallurgist and a domineering martinet. A slave driver, who drove himself as hard as he drove his subordinates, and often spent entire nights working at the Danemere. None of the museum staff would have dared to question what he was up to during those nocturnal sessions, and heaven help them if they had. Moscow was so forceful that even his successor, the literary-minded Mr Swayle, respected a vow to leave the Calamai items alone.

'Ah, this is exactly what I need to jog my memory,' H.-H. took a glass from Lady Lesley and sniffed its contents appreciatively. 'The important thing about Moscow is that he became insane towards the end of his life. A megalomaniac who started to believe that the Danemere's exhibits were his personal property, and like many mental cases he suffered from a persecution complex.

'Fires and thieves and other hazards were threatening his chattels and the security system did not afford complete protection.' The bishop paused and sucked at the plastic straw in his glass. 'Moscow also had another fear, but we'll talk about that later, because it was even more crazy.

'So, from what I've told you, isn't it apparent that the poor, deranged soul decided to transfer Calamai's gold to a place of absolute safety?'

'Where?' Peggy and I, the Booths and Miss Sweeting rapped out the question in unison, but Gerry didn't reply for a moment. He took another pull at the straw and gave a soulful sigh which was as phoney as the Cyclops goblet.

'I don't know the location of Moscow's hiding place. I haven't the slightest idea, but I shall find out, providing you make me an assurance. What I am about to reveal must remain a solemn secret between the six of us, so may I have your promises?'

We all nodded and he sighed even more mournfully. 'Thank you, my friends. How hard it is for a servant of Christ to disobey his Master. How hard for a priest to break his sacred trust and kick against the pricks.

'Still, needs must when the devil drives, so here goes.' The servant of Christ lowered his glass and began the squalid story.

. . . . .

Before leaving England to fleece and enslave our coloured brethren in Africa, Hurst-Hutchins had been a common-or-garden C. of E. canon. In my opinion that's as common as you can get, but there'd been nothing common about Gerry's parish. Saint Egbert's, Worcester Square, was a most exclusive establishment; high-church, high-toned and very high-class. Its flock were *la crème de la crème*, as the frogs say.

The vicar's warden was a duke and the people's warden a viscount. During the first lesson, a retired admiral bellowed out bloodthirsty passages of Hebrew military history as though delivering orders in the teeth of a gale. The second lesson was read more quietly, but just as dramatically, by a world-famous Shakespearian actor. Other celebrities served Gerry at mass, and the brimming collection bags were handed in by a textile millionaire and a Nobel prizewinner.

A rich, successful bunch of worshippers and all piously penitent, which wasn't surprising. You don't gain power and position without committing the odd misdeed and the canon was kept busy doling out absolutions. One of his most tiresome penitents was Tom Moscow.

Sir Thomas Moscow! I couldn't imagine that stern, hanging-judge face registering guilt, but Gerry assured me that my imagination was sub-standard. Moscow had been a regular occupant of the confessional box, though until his final visit he was more troubled by omissions than actual sins.

'I suffer from mistaken charity, Father,' was Sir Thomas's usual opening after the *mea culpa* routine. 'Visitors to the Danemere complained that one of my guides reeked of stale beer while conducting a tour of the museum. I should have dismissed the man immediately, but as he has a wife and six children to support, I shirked my duty and merely issued a reprimand.

'My daughter inherited a wanton streak from her late mother and married an alcoholic. Fortunately he died, but the girl's wantonness persists and so does my moral weakness. Though I am told she is now associating with a criminal degenerate of the lowest type I lack the courage to disown her.

'My assistant curator, Samuel Swayle, is wasting time and energy on writing a worthless book. I have criticized his puerile efforts, but my tongue is not sharp enough to dissuade him.'

Dull, unrewarding stuff, and you couldn't blame the father confessor for becoming a trifle bored. What Father wanted were really juicy admissions. Descriptions of deeds and desires, which could only be pardoned by sincere repentance and cheques made payable to the church restoration fund, a fund administered by the canon in person.

'I'm afraid I was preoccupied by my African venture when Tom Moscow made his last confession to me.' Hurst-Hutchins finished his drink and stifled a belch. 'I also was slightly inebriated, though my breath did not reek, as Moscow described his guide's beery odour. Gin and lemonade are rarely detectable, and Amplex is a sure shield.

'My lack of interest was unforgivable, however, and I never suspected that the poor soul was in genuine need of help and guidance. The session quite slipped from my mind till Colonel Booth happened to mention Moscow's sad end and I realized he'd been serious. That was what made me visit the Calamai collection, and when I saw those retaining brackets the penny started to drop.

'Now, what was actually said at that confessional?' Gerry waited for his memory cells to tick over and warm up. A process which didn't take long. Plenty had been said, though Moscow had done most of the talking, and the talk was confined to questions his adviser was unable to answer with much authority.

'Canon Hurst-Hutchins, as a man of God, do you consider

that certain material objects, such as a saint's relics or a portion of the True Cross, may contain benevolent spiritual forces? Powers to heal the sick and cast out demons?' That was Moscow's lead-line and it had produced a grunt and a noncommittal reference to Lourdes.

'In that case you must believe that other objects can contain the seeds of evil. Satan's vessels spreading disease and destruction across the world.'

'Possibly, my son.' The canon nodded, though he wasn't interested in spiritual powers. His church council had become fractious and the restoration fund was due for an audit. The power of the law was Hurst-Hutchins's worry.

'Then you can advise me, Father.' Moscow leaned forward and even the sozzled confessor sensed his anxiety. 'I have a friend who has been entrusted with a burden which is both holy and accursed. A trust that is rotting his body and his soul, and may soon contaminate other human beings.

'My friend is sick, Father, and he is a lonely man. Apart from myself, the only person he has confided in is a daughter who shares his distress. My friend is too tired to bear his burden any longer, but the trust is a sacred charge. Would it be sinful for him to shed his load? To bury his treasure in a place of safety?'

An unanswerable enquiry unless the canon received more details about the trust and the burden and he was bored with his penitent. He had his own problems and suspected that Moscow was as squiffy as himself. He told Sir Thomas to bring his overloaded pal along to see him at a later date, but the appointment was never confirmed. The restoration-fund auditors arrived the following morning, and Gerry was on his way to Africa before they spotted the first discrepancy in the books.

'How selfish and unfeeling I was! I should have guessed that Moscow was referring to himself and the Calamai treasure and mental instability might lead him to commit two criminal actions. If I had given him comfort and advice the dear man might be alive today and his terrible end will haunt my declining years.

'But I had so many troubles of my own. So many personal crosses to bear.' The ex-vicar clasped his hands in self-pity, but the act was a pantomime and he had little reason to feel sorry for himself. Saint Egbert's church council preferred financial loss to adverse publicity and they had a whip round to balance the accounts. Gerry's pilferings were not reported to the police and he got away scot free.

'As I said the matter quite slipped my mind till you mentioned Moscow's *felo de se*, James.' He looked at Booth and frowned. 'I suppose there is no doubt that it was suicide?'

'None whatsoever. I have told you that three times. Hell's bells, I was a member of the investigating committee, and we soon put paid to that nonsensical murder story.' Jimmy Jackboot turned to me and drew himself up to his full height. A gesture which failed to impress because his full height was under five-and-a-half feet.

'Tom Moscow was friendly with a woman called Hilda Helmer, who vanished at about the same time that he killed himself. Suicide was also the probable cause of her disappearance, but we can't be sure and like the bishop I must ask you and Peggy to regard my information as top secret, Bill.'

We nodded and the colonel acknowledged our promise with a formal bow. 'Hilda Helmer was a boffin employed by the Ministry of Defence. A talented scientist, and a completely ruthless young woman with a persuasive tongue.

'John Butterworth was minister then, and we all know about Butterworth. A pompous ignoramus who revelled in flattery, and Miss Helmer found him easy meat. The fool gave her facilities to conduct a research project in Scotland and he didn't really understand what the project was till it was too late.

'I won't go into details because the whole wretched business was hushed up to avoid public unrest, and rightly so.' Booth clanked back and forth across the room while he spoke. 'The woman's aims were unspeakable and her experiments were oversuccessful and got out of hand. An abominable, atrocious force of evil was created and if the work had continued we'd have suffered national disaster.

'A most disgusting affair which need not concern us, and has nothing to do with our present problem: Calamai's gold.' The colonel blew his nose to express disgust and I marvelled at the workings of a military mind. To kill, torture and mutilate an enemy with conventional weapons is fair play. More sophisticated forms of warfare are unsporting. But, though I despised Booth's sentimentality I shared his disgust, because the business had not been hushed up as effectively as he imagined, and I knew what Miss Helmer's productions were.

'Our concern is with Moscow and these are the facts as I see them.' The colonel replaced his handkerchief and creaked to a halt. 'Because Tom Moscow's corpse was unrecognizable and Hilda Helmer was never found, it was rumoured that Sir Thomas had used a vagrant's body to impersonate his own and the pair had fled to an Iron Curtain country.

'Nonsensical rumours in my view. Miss Helmer was a rash, irresponsible visionary who killed herself in a fit of remorse after realizing what she had produced. Tom Moscow may have been unbalanced, but he had no Marxist leanings and he was no traitor.

'The fellow was as patriotic as I am, and he left written evidence of his intentions. One document was a letter to his lawyer stating that he had contracted an incurable disease and decided to make away with himself. The other was a sealed envelope which the lawyer is to deliver to his daughter when she is capable of collecting it.'

'A letter which has never been collected, Mr Easter, and that is why we need your services.' Lady Lesley was almost civil for a change. 'Moscow's daughter is ill and under medical confinement, and she refuses to discuss her father or his affairs.

'I suppose one should condone the gel's bitterness, though Sir Thomas was not really to blame for her condition. During the inquest their daily help testified that he believed Cathleen was staying with friends and would be away for several days. It was pure bad luck that she returned home unexpectedly and failed to notice the smell of gas.'

'Damned bad luck!' Booth shared his wife's opinion of fortune and I saw that he was staring me hard in the eyes. With the exception of Peg they were all staring at me; Lady L. and Hurst-Hutchins and Miss Sweeting, and I found their stares disturbing. The carpenters were wondering whether my timbers were sound or riddled with rot.

'Yes, damned bad luck for the girl, Bill, but luck hasn't deserted us. We've found someone Cathleen might talk to and we're relying on your persuasive personality, me son.'

'Then you can stop relying on it, Father Courage.' I remembered that Swayle had said Moscow's daughter was locked up in a loony bin. 'I've already impersonated a history professor, and if you think I'm going to do a health-officer act you can dive down the nearest shell-hole.'

'Insolence does not become you, Bill, and no acting should be required. All you have to be is yourself. "A criminal degenerate of the lowest type" was Tom Moscow's description.' The colonel opened a desk drawer and held out a photograph for my inspection. 'Doesn't this ring a bell, Lover Boy?'

It did. The bell's tolls were deafening and I heard the screams and the gibbering again, and felt the knife twist in my guts. Sounds and pains which I'd tried to forget and almost succeeded till Booth's picture revived me. The photograph of a girl who could be ravishingly beautiful in her saner moments. When I'd last seen her she resembled a stricken madonna spouting tears over the hospital pillows and praying that I'd recover from my stab wounds and learn the joys of forgiveness.

Her first prayer had been granted. The second was not, and it never would be.

That lovely, stricken madonna had done the stabbing.

5

Cathleen Moscow . . . Cat Guthrie . . . Cat on the tiles . . . Cat on the Hot Tin Roof. Memories of old, unhappy, far-off things gnawed at my mind as the road carried me back into the past and forward to the future. I tried to dismiss them and concentrate on the present.

During his confession to Hurst-Hutchins, Sir Thomas Moscow had implied that he intended to remove some valuable, but evil, possessions that had been entrusted to him and hide them away for safety's sake. He'd also hinted that his daughter was aware of the plan and that they shared a common illness. Vague, rambling statements which the confessor had ignored at the time, but while Booth was investigating Hilda Helmer's disappearance, more definite facts about Moscow had been unearthed.

On the day he killed himself, Sir Thomas had posted a package to his solicitor containing a covering letter, a suicide note and a sealed envelope addressed to his daughter, Mrs Cathleen Guthrie. The lawyer was instructed to retain that envelope for three years and only hand it over to Mrs Guthrie when she called at his office in person.

The time limit had expired months ago. Almost four years had elapsed since Moscow departed for heaven or hell, but the envelope remained unopened. Sir Thomas had been right in believing that Daughter-Dear-Daughter shared his illness. Cathleen Moscow, as she had been registered at birth, couldn't visit the solicitor's office to collect anything. Mrs Cat Guthrie, as I'd known her, was locked up in a mental institution called Normanton Towers. Her jailor's name was Dr Cyrus Toylar. Her condition was known as Toylar's Syndrome.

A condition which caused reticence and bad temper. Cat refused to answer questions about Moscow and shunned visitors. When Booth had called at the asylum and tried to pump her with a 'close friend of your dear father' approach, she'd told him to go to hell. One couldn't blame her for that, but how would she respond to a friend of her own – an old flame?

We'd know soon enough, because the flame was on the way to Normanton Towers with his sister, Miss Margaret Easter, sitting beside him. Sitting rather too closely for comfort. Peggy's massive thigh kept pressing against the gear lever of the little Italian sports car Lady Lesley had lent us and I drove slowly; partly for safety's sake and partly to consider the past, present and future.

The past was unpleasant, the future uncertain, but the present was proceeding smoothly, and Toylar's secretary had passed on my telephone enquiry. Would Mrs Guthrie be prepared to see Mr William Easter, a former admirer who had been abroad for some years and only just discovered her whereabouts? Mrs Guthrie had responded enthusiastically. She was not merely prepared to see the admirer, she was counting the hours and minutes for our reunion and instructed the secretary to blow a kiss down the line. A gesture which must have embarrassed the woman as much as it did me.

However hard I tried to forgive and forget, the memories returned and the scar tissue on my belly started to throb.

I'd never known that Cat was old Moscow's daughter. She never mentioned a family and, when she said that our horrible love nest belonged to Daddy, I thought she'd neglected to add the prefix *Sugar*. I met Cat because I was pally with her husband and, whatever Moscow had said, Michael Guthrie wasn't a lush. Mike was just an unfortunate chap who liked his booze, but couldn't hold it. I was with him and his missus when he stumbled in front of that bus in Piccadilly, and he'd only drunk five pints of beer. One of the rozzers suggested that I might have pushed him in the interests of romance, but the accusation was a lie. Cat and I were merely acquaintances then, I hadn't laid a finger on her, and we didn't become lovers till Mike was decently cremated. I remember watching his smoke drift from the chimney before we went to the hotel for our romp. An exciting romp, because Mike had left quite a widow. The face of an angel, the body of a petite Miss World, the appetite of . . .

I'm trying to think of a few famous nymphomaniacs, but only Messalina comes to mind, and I bet Cat could have knocked spots off her. Angel Face Puss was insatiable, though that didn't bother me for a while. I've been blessed with a strong constitution and thoroughly enjoyed our first month of cohabitation, as Lady Lesley would have phrased it.

But even the best things pall and you can't eat caviare for every meal of the day. My loved one was too demanding. She was also too possessive, and I don't like being possessed. If I wanted a night out with the boys, Cat would tag along. If I came back late from a business deal, there'd be hell to pay. If I failed to satisfy her I'd receive ridicule, invective and abuse. Before a second month had passed I realized she was crazy and decided to quit.

The escape attempt took place in a dreary corner of north-west Scotland and the prison was equally dreary. Daddy's cottage had been designed by someone with no idea of taste or comfort, and a fondness for local tradition and gothic decor. The bedroom's tartan wallpaper and moth-eaten stags' heads made my sexual labours even more arduous, and the living-room walls had been left bare and unplastered to display 'them gran' Hieland stanes'. The roof leaked, the smouldering peat fire produced far more smoke than heat, and there was a particularly gruesome metal plaque cemented to the chimney breast. The image of a Gorgon which seemed to be scowling at me whenever I was in eyeshot of it.

That was my Dartmoor, but conditions appeared favourable on the night I decided to break out. Gusts of snow and sleet were rattling the windows, and my get-away car, an ageing Rover coupé with a fractured exhaust, was waiting. Cat had a dose of flu. Not a severe dose unfortunately, and her temperature was only ninety-nine. But she suffered from hypochondria as well as nymphomania and was suitably worried when I frowned at the thermometer and pronounced a reading of a hundred and three. A doctor was required, but for some reason the nearest G.P.'s telephone was out of order and Cat refused to be left alone while I went up the glen to fetch him. Self-help was our sole salvation and remedies were to hand: aspirin, whisky and a hot mustard bath. Plenty of aspirin, plenty of whisky, and the bath I ran for Cat was almost scalding. She should have dozed off in the water, but as our crofter neighbours frequently remarked in the local pub, 'The best-laid schemes o' mice and men gang aft agley.' My scheme was perfectly laid. My transport let me down.

I helped Cat into the bath, told her to call out when she'd had a good, long soak, and then packed my belongings and a few of hers. I didn't take any jewellery, but she did owe me something for the back-breaking services I'd rendered her, and she wouldn't starve for the lack of the credit card and the fifteen pounds I tucked into my wallet. Cat was well-breached financially and well-developed physically. I felt no guilt or anxiety when I closed the cottage door behind me and crossed to the car.

Rovers are excellent vehicles, but my coupé was past its prime and had received harsh treatment. The battery was low, the starter brushes were worn, and there was no response when I turned the ignition switch. Frustrating, but not deflating. As de Gaulle explained after being booted out of *la Belle France*, I had lost a battle, not a war, and victory would still be gained. The old car was provided with a crank handle and one quick heave did the trick. The engine roared to life and I removed the crank with a song of triumph in my heart. That healthy, pulsing roar was like a hymn in praise of liberty and the path to freedom lay ahead. I believe that I actually did sing as I hurried back to the driving seat, but I can't recall what the ditty was. All I can remember clearly is pain and the face of pain's deliverer.

The Rover's broken exhaust pipe had given the show away because its roar was too pulsing, too lively, too triumphant. Cat had heard the commotion and realized that her captive was escaping. She had leapt from the bath, screaming and gibbering, and grabbed a carving knife on her way to the door. I saw its blade glitter in the moonlight, but did nothing till it was too late. Her naked, snow-flecked body made me think of a fairy-tale ice-maiden. Her expression was as chilling and ferocious as the fireplace Gorgon.

Chilling, ferocious and hypnotic, and the knife shot forward before I came to my senses and flailed at her with the crank handle. My blow missed – Cat's didn't. She damned near killed me.

Alas, poor Cat. She was very repentant at the hospital, and though the police wanted to book her for grievous bodily harm, I refused to press charges. A nurse had found her credit card in my wallet, and there'd have been awkward questions to answer had the case gone to court. I told somebody called the Procurator Fiscal that Cat was feverish when she attacked me and the assault had arisen during a lovers' tiff. The Fiscal didn't believe the story, but he had to accept it, and I left the country as soon as my stitches were removed. Apart from a brief mention in one of the Scottish papers the event aroused little public interest and, before Booth showed me that photograph, it had almost vanished from my memory.

But not from Miss Janet Sweeting's memory. Aunty Jan had a mind like a filing cabinet and she'd read that newspaper snippet and stored it away in her brain box for over three years. When the Calamai project was discussed, ex-Commander Sweeting realized that there was an inquisitor who might be able to make Cat talk. A Prince Charming to arouse Sleeping Beauty with his kiss.

Sleeping Beauty. We had entered Normanton village and I turned the steering wheel reluctantly as Peg pointed out a sign post directing us towards the Towers. Booth had assured me that plastic surgery had worked miracles, but his brief interview had taken place in a dimly-lit room, and I wondered what Cat looked like now. Certainly not as lovely as the girl I'd known, because her injuries had been considerable. Fate and coincidence are cruel enemies at times. Cat had gone home to Daddy on the evening Moscow killed himself.

Most suicide attempts fail because they're planned to fail, exhibitionist acts intended to arouse sympathy and draw attention to yourself. Pleas for help, so that you can cry on Matron's shoulder after she's pumped out the poison, and tell Doctor how neglected and unhappy you are. Sir Thomas Moscow didn't want sympathy. He'd decided to die and he left nothing to chance.

Moscow's house was supplied with town gas in those days. A chemical which provides a clean, inexpensive journey to death, but death itself was not good enough for Sir Thomas. Moscow had delusions of grandeur and wished to return to his maker in style. Three petrol drums were dragged into the kitchen to fuel his Viking's funeral, and he fitted the drums with detonators timed to go off shortly after he was dead.

An impressive display of megalomania which started the rumours of a faked suicide Booth had mentioned; suspicions that another body had been blown to Valhalla while Moscow and Miss Helmer headed for the Iron Curtain.

Nonsensical tosh, in Booth's opinion, and he and his fellow sleuths had checked the evidence and fancied they knew the exact sequence of events.

After posting the package to his lawyer, Moscow had had a shave and a bath and swallowed an overdose of barbiturates to make assurance doubly sure. He had then walked down to the kitchen, closed the windows and ventilators and positioned a mat against the door. The room must have been virtually airtight after he'd set the detonator timers, turned on the oven taps and placed his head in the stove. A spectacular, well-planned exit designed to harm no one except its perpetrator, and Moscow was unaware that Cat had lost her criminal degenerate and was hurrying home to sob in Daddy's shoulder.

When Cat arrived home, she imagined Daddy was out and decided that a cup of tea might cheer her up. When she opened the kitchen door, the detonator switches clicked. When she stepped into the kitchen, gas and petrol exploded.

Sir Thomas Moscow could only be identified by fragments of his false teeth which were found imbedded in the walls. Cat was thrown back by the blast and escaped the blaze that destroyed the house, but she was pretty badly damaged when the fireman found her and the damage was not only physical. After the surgeons finished their operations she'd been transferred to Dr Toylar's private Broadmoor and had remained there ever since. A reticent patient who did not welcome visitors, though she was prepared to receive a guest. Sir Galahad had forgiven his murderess damsel and was returning to renew his troth.

And Galahad had arrived. I stopped the car outside a lodge gate facing the village green and Normanton Towers was in view. A rather disappointing view, because the name was boastful. Though Dr Toylar's establishment was fronted by a lawn and a flower garden, no towers or battlements loomed above them and the building was less than a hundred years old. A large, three-storeyed box of red brick, which had probably been designed for some Victorian magnate who'd successfully ground the faces of the poor, but shunned flamboyance. The edifice was as dull and orthodox as they come and typical of the period. You can find dozens of similar examples dotted around the Home Counties and most of them have been converted into hospitals, hotels or sports clubs.

Normanton Towers certainly resembled a sports club on the surface, and though it was late autumn the weather was warm and various sports were in progress: clock golf and croquet and other less energetic recreations. Three men and a woman were playing cards on a table beneath a cedar tree, a man in a deckchair was doing a crossword, another man was engrossed with a jigsaw puzzle.

Dr Toylar's patients appeared contented and respectable enough, and though the lodge-keeper had the torso of a muscle-bound gorilla, he acted like any well-trained club servant; courteous and deferential, but wary of interlopers.

'One moment please, Mr Easter.' The gorilla bowed politely when I introduced myself and said we were expected. But he wasn't admitting any gate-crashers and he told us to wait while he phoned through to the office. During the interval I studied the friendly club-like scene and saw that it was a sham. The house windows were barred and the tall railings surrounding the grounds were topped with barbarous devices which I'd only seen at a public school and a maximum-security prison. Steel-spiked rollers which would revolve and slice you open if you tried to climb them.

Normanton Towers was almost as well guarded as the Danemere Museum, and everything in Dr Toylar's garden was not as lovely as it had first appeared. Three more muscular attendants, two men and a woman, were stationed in strategic positions to keep a watchful eye on their charges' activities and it was soon apparent that muscle and watchfulness were needed. The clock golfers were behaving rather too exuberantly and they were all poor losers. Every successful shot was loudly applauded, but when one player missed a hole he threw down his putter and stalked petulantly off the green. The card quartet were equally excitable, and the crossword puzzler resented failure. A clue had foxed him and shortly before the porter opened the gate for us I heard a curse and saw him tear the paper into shreds.

But it was a croquet competitor who presented the real danger. Her ball had been *stymied*, or whatever the term is, and she was squinting around to solve the problem when she saw me and I heard another cry of emotion. A joyous whoop which rang like a view-hallo and was followed by a frenzied dash towards the car; face beaming, mallet raised in welcome.

A welcome which vanished abruptly when she noticed that Peggy's hand was on my knee. The beam changed to a glare, the whoop became a snarl of hatred, the mallet swung out like a club.

Peggy only avoided death because the nurses acted with commendable speed. The heavy croquet mallet was within inches of her skull before a karate chop knocked it aside and a flying rugger tackle brought the assailant crashing to earth.

After Peg's would-be murderess was under control, trussed and pinioned and deprived of a weapon, I saw that Booth had told the truth and no scars were visible on the crazed, contorted features. Plastic surgery had worked wonders on a face, but I couldn't say the same about Dr Toylar's efforts to cure a mind.

Cat Guthrie had become a real cat. Her eyes glowed as though there were lamps behind them.

6

'A regrettable incident, but you have only yourselves to blame.' Half an hour had elapsed since Cat had been frogmarched into the house and Dr Cyrus Toylar paced a balcony flanking his office.

'Strange as it seems, Cathleen Guthrie has remained in love with you, Mr Easter. The news that you were coming here produced the first sign of happiness she has shown for years, which is the reason I agreed to your visit. I thought you might be able to help my patient, but quite the opposite occurred.' He gave me a scowl that would have quelled a ward of rebellious homicidal maniacs. 'Why the hell didn't you have the common sense to tell us you were bringing a sister with you? Cathleen imagined Miss Easter was your wife and her joy changed to jealousy and insane hatred.

'Regrettable and irresponsible behaviour, though I'm sorry if the display of violence caused you distress, Madam.' The doctor's expression softened as he turned to Peg, but distress was too mild a word to describe her feelings. Peggy was still trembling like the proverbial aspen leaf; a spectacular sight. And so would you tremble if you'd almost had your brains battered to pulp.

'However, all's well that ends well, and no real harm has been done, thanks to prompt action by Smith and Hackworth.' Toylar leaned over the balustrade and nodded at the two gorillas who had dashed to our rescue. Cat's demonstration had created some unrest among her fellow patients, but peace was restored to the garden, and the female attendant was handing out cups of tea.

'But without prompt action, your stupidity might have caused a serious riot, Mr Easter. Some of my guests are quite unpredictable, and one fit of the tantrums can trigger off others. If they weren't blessed with private means or wealthy relations half of those people would be in state asylums for the criminally insane.' The doctor's rich bass voice made me think of war drums throbbing through a jungle, and his complexion strengthened the image. Apart from a mop of curly grey hair, Cyrus Toylar was as black as a policeman's boot.

'Psychos and schizoids . . . paranoids and pyromaniacs . . . kleptomaniacs and manic depressives. We've got just about the lot at Normanton Towers, Mr Easter, and if you named a mental aberration, I could probably show you an example.

'Mine is a rewarding profession scientifically, though not financially nowadays. Many of our patients depend on fixed incomes to pay their fees, and with inflation at its present level . . .' He shrugged and clicked his tongue abjectly, but the suggestion of poverty was unimpressive. His wild-silk suit must have cost at least two hundred pounds and the pearl on his tie pin was as big as a processed pea. The tie under the pin denoted membership of the El Vagabondo Club, which is a most exclusive and expensive establishment to belong to. Hurst-Hutchins had once tried to join and had been turned down flat. Dr Cyrus Toylar might have started to feel the pinch, but he'd been on to a damned good thing.

'I mustn't waste time with personal problems, however, so let's go inside and discuss the patient I'd hoped you could help.' He straightened from the rail and squared his shoulders, and I did find that gesture impressive. Far more impressive than the way old Booth had straightened, because Toylar was a much bigger man, and shot and shrapnel had not marred his physique. Though slightly past the prime of life, he was almost seven feet tall and in the pink of condition.

Pink is a stupid way to describe a Negro's colouring but the doctor's colour was a thing of beauty. His skin glistened like those plastic rubbish bags issued by the council when there's a dustmen's strike and you have to dispose of your own garbage.

'My patient, and your former fiancée, Mr Easter.' He had led us back into the office which was as opulent as his appearance and halted beside a *Louis Seize* desk. 'Poor Cathleen Guthrie who worships you as she used to worship her father. Cathleen rarely mentions Sir Thomas now, but she once thought he was a god. That's why she followed his instructions to put herself in my care before her symptoms started.

'Of course Cathleen didn't tell you that Moscow was her father, Mr Easter.' Toylar shook his head when I questioned him. 'Such an admission would have been a betrayal of trust, and you might have pried into their relationship, which was not a healthy one.

'No not healthy at all; a most squalid association.' He turned and stared at me again. Another hard professional stare that commenced at my feet and moved slowly upwards, studying my stance and my torso, and making me feel naked and bloody uncomfortable. When his eyes reached mine they seemed to bore into them and I asked him what the hell he was looking for.

'Signs of illness, Mr Easter, but I'm glad to say that none are apparent on the surface. Not that I really expected to see them after such a long passage of time. It must be almost four years since you and Cathleen parted company.' He nodded reassuringly, but the stare continued as though he was examining a noxious bacterium through a microscope.

'Yes, you seem to be in fair physical condition, but what about the brain and the central nervous system? Do you suffer from sudden memory lapses, muscular tremors, or unwarranted spasms of anger? Any symptoms resembling V.D.?'

'I do not, Doctor, though I'm beginning to be angry now.' I wished that history could be pushed back and the brute's circumstances suited to his name. It was pleasant to imagine Cyrus Toylar toiling away in the Mississippi cotton fields with a whip behind him. 'My sister and I came here to see Mrs Guthrie and my state of health is no concern of yours.'

'I hope you're right, sir. I sincerely hope that you're right, and you probably are. Mental degeneration would have started by now.' At long last he looked away from me and addressed Peggy. 'What I am going to say will naturally shock you, Madam, but if you and Mr Easter wish to help Cathleen, I must make the position clear.

'Toylar's Syndrome, as medical journals have been kind enough to call the condition, is a progressive illness caused by a viral organism which I have isolated, but failed to destroy. Though I hope to do so some day.' The isolator of the disease spoke with pride. 'At the moment there is no medical cure whatsoever. The organism resists all the known antibiotics, and intense cold appears to encourage its growth. Only three forces can halt infection and two of them are useless. Heat strong enough to kill the victim, and time.' He paused and opened a silver cigar box on the desk. 'Isotope tests prove that the virus will become senile and harmless in approximately one hundred years.

'But a hundred years is too long to save poor Cathleen Guthrie, and before discussing the third means of defence, I would like to tell you how the disease cycle runs.' Toylar took a Double Corona from his case and closed the lid. Though I enjoy a good cigar, the mean bastard didn't think of offering me one.

'Six people have contracted Toylar's Syndrome to date and with the exception of Cathleen and one fortunate man they all committed suicide.' He sniffed the Corona and snapped on the flame of a gold cigarette lighter engraved with his initials and the El Vagabondo crest.

'You can't blame Moscow and the others for killing themselves – I might have done the same thing in the circumstances.' The cigar was drawing nicely and Toylar blew a smoke ring while crossing to a filing cabinet. 'The early symptoms of disease are psychological and akin to paranoia. Jealousy, possessiveness and delusions of persecution leading to a power complex and uncontrollable rages.

'You recently experienced such a rage, Madam.' He bowed to Peggy and unlocked the cabinet. 'Sir Thomas Moscow believed he was being haunted by some long dead Italian artist. Cathleen considers that I am an ogre who tortures and oppresses her.

'All these people suffered from paranoia, before their physical decline began, but as I said one man escaped and he is still alive.' The doctor dragged at his cigar again and a second smoke ring drifted to the ceiling. 'The man's own resistance checked the physical illness and sadism saved his mind. He vented his spite on animals.

'An unpleasant method of escape, but sublimation is a common factor in paranoia. Nagging wives and bullying employers are less troublesome if you can kill them in your brain. If you are Hitler or Stalin or . . .' he paused to think of another despot and settled for a compatriot, 'Chaka the Terrible.

'The man's conviction that animals were his enemies set up a chemical reaction that stimulated the hormones and antibodies in his own system and they turned on the attackers.

'Cathleen Guthrie once had an equally strong conviction, Mr Easter, and it might . . . just might help her, if you are prepared to co-operate with me.

'Good – very good.' I'd promised my total cooperation, and though Toylar's back was towards us I could see his smile reflected on the cabinet top.

'Thomas Moscow left his daughter very little money, but when she first came here she suffered from delusions of wealth. A day-dream that she was the heiress to some enormous treasure. I failed to encourage that dream and lost her confidence, as I have told you. Cathleen refuses to discuss the matter with me, but she might confide in you.' He opened one of the cabinet drawers and brought out a cardboard folder. 'If she does mention her illusions I beg you to pander to them and give me a full report of everything she says. Indulgence is the sole way to tame an insane monster. A physical monster at the end, Mr Easter, and the final symptoms are too terrible to be borne.'

Toylar hadn't noticed my excitement at his references to Calamai and the treasure, and he produced a photograph from the folder. 'By experimenting with small animals and accelerating the disease cycle artificially, I have managed to construct an identikit picture of what Moscow and my other patients would look like if they hadn't done away with themselves. What Cathleen Guthrie may soon look like. What your brother might have looked like if his affair with Cathleen had been more prolonged, Miss Easter.

'Excuse me for a moment, though.' The telephone rang as he was about to hand the photograph to Peg and he picked it up and grunted into the mouthpiece. 'Dr Toylar here.

'Ah, thanks, Matron.' The message was brief and he slammed down the instrument. 'Cathleen has had your relationship explained to her and is ready to see you. She is quite calm and mildly sedated and you needn't worry about catching her illness. Though I have failed to kill the virus, drugs have slowed the advance and rendered it sterile to other potential victims.

'But before you go to Cathleen's room, I want you to appreciate how bleak her future is unless you can help her. Hope is the poor girl's sole salvation, Mr Easter, so foster those hopes. Talk about gold. Ask her about Moscow's treasure.' He held out the photograph and I heard Peggy gasp as she looked at it.

'That's the final result of the disease, and the virus is transmitted by two methods. The first is through injection into the blood stream. The second is through sexual intercourse. The reason I enquired about your health, Mr Easter.

'No, the end product is not very pretty, and neither is the beginning of the story.' It was my turn to examine the photograph, and though I didn't gasp or cry out my eyes seemed to blur and a roaring sound in my head almost drowned Toylar's voice.

'Sir Thomas Moscow lacked morality and Cathleen worshipped him as she worships you.' The doctor grinned at the horror on my face. '"The sins of the fathers are visited on their children", Mr Easter.

'Moscow's sins and his sickness were visited on Cathleen by incest.'

'Try to forgive me, Bill. Please . . . please try.' As Toylar had promised, tranquillizers and an explanation by the matron had worked wonders and Cat was the soul of contrition.

'You never told me that you had a sister, Bill, and when I saw Margaret in the car I thought she was your wife. I thought you'd stopped loving me and this was just a social call or an act of charity.' Cat lay on a bed and, though tears had reddened her eyes, they had ceased to glow and I could see little resemblance to the crazed, screaming creature who had brandished the croquet mallet. I had rarely seen Cat Guthrie look more beautiful and there was no hint that Toylar's prophecy would be fulfilled, though his identikit mock-up was sickening. The deformed body, the bloated, wrinkled flesh . . . the tumours.

'No, I must be truthful, darling.' She dabbed her cheeks with a tissue. 'I thought you might have come to mock me . . . to laugh at a poor prisoner who once injured you. How stupid and foolish I was, Margaret.' She looked at Peggy and in spite of the tears her eyes were as appealing as they'd been on the day Mike Guthrie was cremated. 'I was longing for Bill's visit. I've been counting every minute and every hour since they said he was coming. And then, when I saw you I behaved like . . .' I thought she was about to say, 'like a lunatic', but she checked herself, '. . . like an animal.'

'Stop crying, Cat. There's nothing to cry about any more. We forgive you.' My assurance was part-truth and part-lie. She was a lunatic and I could forgive the assault on poor Peggy. But I'd never condone her relationship with Moscow; never in a thousand years. The image of Cat in the arms of her father . . . the knowledge that I'd shared her with that grim hanging judge . . . the possibility that she might have contaminated me with his loathsome complaint . . .

But I was beginning to have doubts. Toylar had said that Moscow admitted their incest shortly before he killed himself, but Toylar had also said that one of the disease-symptoms was fantasy. Sir Thomas Moscow had been an intolerant, guilt-ridden puritan. Had he referred to desire rather than the actual deed?

He who looked after a woman in lust hath already committed adultery with her in his heart. Though I may have misquoted the text slightly, I know my Bible as well as Bishop Gerald Hurst-Hutchins and Dr Cyrus Toylar, M.D. (Lagos), Dip.Psych. (Lusaka), Ph.D. (Bandalog). Mental lust could have been Moscow's confession.

'Thank you, Bill, and God bless you, Margaret.' Cat reached for her new-found sister's hand, but Peggy drew back from the bed. Courage is not one of Peg's virtues, and though Toylar had promised us that the germs were sterile, she wasn't taking any chances.

'Yes, God bless you both, and He will bless you. He will bless you and reward you, because God brought you back to me, Bill. You and Margaret are God's instruments sent here to help me.' Contrition changed to conviction and Cat spoke with the absolute assurance of the mentally deranged. 'God has ordered you to get me out of this cell . . . this bloody, stinking, unprintable prison.'

She grimaced around the room, and though there was no stink to speak of, I saw that it was a cell. The bed and the wardrobe and every article of furniture were clamped to the floor. A fine view of the Surrey hills was partially screened by the window bars, and a nurse had locked the door behind us and told me to ring a bell when our interview was over. The only other exit was a skylight in the ceiling, which wasn't a feasible route unless you had a ladder or could jump like a kangaroo.

And if you did reach the skylight and climb on to the roof there'd be small profit in the exercise. Cat's dungeon was on the top floor, the patients were watched by guards who had already proved their efficiency, and spiked rollers surrounded the grounds. Normanton Towers would be a difficult prison to escape from, and I asked Cat why an escape was necessary. She was an invalid needing medical treatment and she had every creature comfort.

'Because I'm not sick, Bill; not any longer. Surely you can see that?' My question was intended to provoke and it produced a puzzled frown. 'I was ill once. That's why I obeyed my father's instructions and appealed to Toylar. Why I've rotted here for over three years; the prisoner of a sadist, a murderous ogre who uses me as a guinea pig.' She pulled up the sleeve of her bedjacket and we saw that her arm was spotted with hypodermic punctures.

'Toylar is a murderer, Bill. He murdered my father. He murdered them all; Hilda and Blake, Rolfe and Healy. Toylar drove them mad and that's why they killed themselves. He tried to destroy me too, but he failed. I conquered the disease and I'm sane. I'm as sane as you and Margaret.

'I'm clever too, Bill. I'm clever and rich and God is on my side.' She closed her eyes for a moment and I could almost hear her brain cells creak in concentration. 'God sent me a visitor the other day. A funny, little crippled man who said he was a friend of Daddy's, but I didn't believe him. I told him to go away.' Her eyes opened wide and she shook her head irritably. 'I was wrong of course. That cripple came from God and he realized I was cured. He reported back to God, and that's why you were sent here to release me.'

Cat's convictions regarding the deity were both frightening and pathetic, and the funny, little crippled man had not reported any cure to his Lord of Hosts. Colonel Wellington Booth considered she was a dangerous lunatic and the croquet mallet affray had proved him right. No escape attempt was in the offing, and Peg and I were merely intended to gain Cat's confidence. To pump her about Moscow in the hope that he might have made some statement regarding the treasure.

'I'm sane and I'm rich, Bill. As rich as Croesus, and you and Margaret are going to share my riches.' Pumping was unnecessary and Cat raised the subject herself. She also raised her hand to mine and, unlike Peg, I didn't draw back, though if I'd been a dog my hackles would have bristled. Her fingers were icy, their nails dug into my palm, and I seemed to feel the knife blade stabbing my guts and see the mallet swinging at Peg. I also seemed to see the face of Sir Thomas Moscow watching me from behind Cat's eyes, and for an instance I imagined that Moscow's voice spoke to us.

'Yes, we're all going to be rich, my darlings, and this is why.' At long last she released her grip and I withdrew my aching hand. 'Daddy said he left me a legacy, but I didn't realize what it was till that little limping man put the idea into my mind.

'I know now, though. I know that I'm an heiress with a great treasure waiting to be claimed. My only problem is to escape from here and that's why God sent you and Peggy, Bill.' Cat glanced at the door to make sure that the nurse wasn't watching us through the tiny Judas window in its middle panel.

'Not a conventional escape, Bill. Ladders and files and hacksaws won't be required – all I need is a champion with the courage to rescue his damsel in distress. Lancelot, Perceval, Jack the Giant Killer, or . . .' Cat paused, and once again I saw Moscow's face behind her eyes. 'No, I'm afraid I can't remember any hero called Sir William, but you're the damsel's champion now, darling. You're my ogre slayer, and you'll have to work for your share of Calamai's treasure.' She gave a tinkling laugh that made my flesh crawl.

'Billy the Butcher is going to kill Cyrus Toylar.'

7

'Cyrus Toylar appears to be an objectionable fellow, but I don't see how killing him would solve the problem.' We had returned to Booth's H.Q. and Hurst-Hutchins was reviewing the situation. 'Mrs Guthrie is a certified lunatic motivated by spite and hatred. If Toylar died and Normanton Towers closed down, the patients would be transferred to another institution and we'd gain nothing.

'Sad for Mrs Guthrie . . . irritating for us.' The bishop sighed and glanced at our fellow conspirators. Lady Lesley and Miss Sweeting were standing beside a window and Gretchen the German domestic had been included in the gathering. She and Booth were bent over a desk piled with papers and photographs and didn't appear to be listening to a word Gerry said.

'Exceedingly irritating, and the woman is probably right in describing herself as a human guinea pig. Toylar is cursed with ambition and he hopes to win acclaim by discovering a cure for the disease which already bears his name. Medical science can lead to sadism at times.

'But Mrs Guthrie's woes are not our concern and we must assess the facts.' Though it was early November the weather had become warm and sultry and the bishop pulled out a handkerchief to mop his sweating brow. 'After her father's death Mrs Guthrie suffered a nervous breakdown and asked to be committed to Toylar's care. The committal orders were signed by the necessary authorities and they can only be revoked when Toylar and an independent board of specialists certify that the woman has regained her sanity and is ready to face the world.

'A pronouncement which will never be made. It is clear from what Bill and Peggy have said that the patient is a potential murderess, but Dr Toylar also has another reason for keeping her in custody. Tom Moscow left Toylar an annuity and a legacy. The annuity is to be paid as long as Cathleen remains at Normanton

Towers. The legacy will become Toylar's absolute property if and when she is declared sane.' Hurst-Hutchins replaced his handkerchief and sighed again. 'A ticklish situation, my friends. There is no legal way of releasing the woman, and in Bill Easter's opinion, Normanton Towers is escape-proof.'

'I'm not concerned with trivial legalities or amateur opinions, Gerald.' At long last Booth looked up from the table. 'I have only one question to put to you, Bill, and it has nothing to do with the asylum's security arrangements.' He stared at me and in spite of his insolence it wasn't an unfriendly stare. The kind of quizzical appraisal a commanding officer might give to a subaltern who has crawled back from no-man's-land with information that can lead to victory or rout. A path through the mine field? An enemy ruse to lure his advance towards their guns? 'Do you believe that the woman told you the truth about her father's treasure, or was she merely romancing?'

'How the hell should I know, Colonel?' The word amateur had rankled and I glared back at him. 'I am not a psychiatrist and I can only repeat what she said.' I summarized Cat's statements for the second time. 'Shortly before he killed himself Thomas Moscow instructed his daughter to contact Toylar if she experienced any symptoms of mental illness. He also hinted that he had left her something of immense value, but it could not be claimed till three years had passed and she was in a position to collect an envelope from Moscow's lawyers; Messrs Harlow, Haddock & Clap.' Under normal circumstances I'd have found the firm's name amusing, but I didn't smile and neither did my audience. Even Peg was eyeing me intently, though she had heard the story from Cat's mouth.

'Mrs Guthrie hadn't a clue what Moscow's treasure trove was until another amateur approached her.' It was my turn to sneer, and I was glad to see Booth wince slightly. 'You suggested that Moscow referred to the Calamai collection, Colonel, and Cathleen believed you. She also believes that the time is ripe for her to claim her inheritance and considers that she is as sane as . . .' I didn't have to think of an example of lunacy because one was facing me. 'As sane as yourself, Colonel Wellington Booth.'

'Thank you, my boy, but the comparison is inapt, and I am not sane. Like many men of action, I am blessed with divine mania; a force which Gretchen would call *das Geist.*' Jimmy Jackboot hadn't realized I was ribbing him and he patted Brünnhilde's arm.

'Mrs Guthrie's mention of a document confirms my suspicions, however, and we have already tried to acquire that document. After I'd spoken to Cathleen Guthrie, Janet Sweeting paid Harlow, Haddock & Clap a visit and Mr Haddock admitted its existence.'

'A fruitless visit, I'm afraid, and Mr Haddock is a difficult person to deal with.' Aunty Jan spoke sadly, as though a favourite nephew had neglected to send her a Christmas card. 'Though I had a note of authorization bearing an exact copy of Mrs Guthrie's signature, the man was adamant. Sir Thomas Moscow had instructed that the envelope could only be given to his daughter in person, and I can see no hope of deceiving Haddock with an impersonator as he knows Mrs Guthrie well.

'A raid on Haddock's premises is impractical too. The envelope is lodged in a vault with several thousand other documents. Even if the vault could be entered it might take ages to find the item we need, Colonel.

'Unless . . .' A pleasant thought had occurred to her and Aunty's expression brightened. 'Perhaps Mr Haddock could be persuaded to co-operate, sir.'

'I will not tolerate torture except as a last extreme, Janet. This is what I intend to do.' Booth gave his blonde henchwoman another affectionate pat and marched over to the drink cupboard.

'We know that Tom Moscow did substitute fakes for the Calamai collection, and we shall assume that his letter to Mrs Guthrie states where the original pieces are hidden. We shall admit that Mrs Guthrie is a necessary ally and act accordingly.' The little upstart pointed at a calendar. 'Cathleen Guthrie must be released from her place of confinement and the escape will be achieved next Wednesday, which happens to be November 5th.' He opened the cupboard and produced a formidable array of bottles.

'Guy Fawkes and Solomon Barnsby are on our side, and so are the elements.' Though I hadn't heard of the said Barnsby, Booth's tone radiated confidence and I almost forgave him for calling me an amateur.

'Fireworks will help to screen our assault and the long-range weather forecast suggests that the night will be dark and cloudy. Normanton Towers has several defences, but there is one weakness which makes Toylar's guards and fences and alarm systems laughable.

'Mrs Guthrie's cell has a skylight and we shall attack from the sky.' He cackled to emphasize how pathetic Toylar's defences were. 'While Gerald was talking, Fräulein Schmidt and I have been working out a plan, and given skill, courage and military discipline, I do not believe we could fail.

'But the scheme is yours, Gretchen, and I want a definite promise.' He motioned Brünnhilde to her feet. 'Can it be done?'

It could be done. We were assured of success in no uncertain terms and, after the Teutonic Maid Marian had finished outlining the plan, I felt like singing 'For she's a jolly good fellow.'

'I have the honour to be distantly related to Hanna Reitsch, who piloted a Fieseler-Storch monoplane from Berlin's Ost-West-Axis during the height of the Soviet bombardment.' She spoke with a deal of pride and I didn't blame her. I was familiar with Hanna Reitsch's exploits and admired them.

If Hitler hadn't been a stubborn nut case, little Miss Reitsch could have flown him away from the Russians and given the sod breathing space. Over a year's supply of breath and a formal trial before the Americans hanged him. I bet he'd have enjoyed his trial too, and he might have been acquitted without a stain on his character. Adolf possessed the gift of the gab and I was acquitted once because I had a barrister who could have made a fortune on the stage. 'Crucified, pilloried, hounded and martyred,' was how he described my plight, and three jury women were sobbing before he finished his final appeal on my behalf. Emotional oratory can always sway fools and if you doubt that you'd better read a few court reports.

'Apart from my ancestry, I am a qualified pilot myself and all we require is a plane.' Gretchen squared her shoulders and bowed to Booth. 'A suitable volunteer is available.'

I was glad to hear about the volunteer and my spirits warmed towards the Fräulein when Booth assured us that he could lay on a helicopter and she detailed the attack. Fireworks banging away to drown the sound of the chopper, which would be hidden in cloud. A winch lowering one of Booth's stalwarts (probably an ex-parachute wallah) on to the asylum roof. A chisel prising open the skylight, and Cat hauled to freedom in a bos'n's chair.

So obvious and simple, but strokes of genius should not be praised till their success is proved and I complimented the genius prematurely.

'Thank you, Mr Easter.' She bowed again and smiled smugly. 'I am glad you approve, but there is one thing I must emphasize.' The smile faded and she frowned at the glass of whisky Booth had given me. 'Steady nerves will be needed for the operation and that drink must be your last.' She glanced at her watch and did some mental arithmetic. 'I shall be dropping you through the skylight in exactly eighty-seven hours' time.'

8

It had to be me. Though I'd been tense and resentful before climbing into the helicopter, a couple of purple heart tablets had given me courage and I knew that Gretchen Schmidt was right. After she took off my spirits soared with the machine and I felt quite confident while we thundered through the night.

Yes, it had to be me, because Cat Guthrie was so unstable that she wouldn't trust any other rescuer. She would probably scream her head off if a stranger appeared at the skylight and bring Toylar or his gorilla guards bursting through the door. Only Darling Bill could be relied on and I wasn't complaining. The risks were great, but so were the rewards, and though Jimmy Jackboot might be as mad as Cat I couldn't criticize his organization or his generosity.

The chopper was a Mark 12 Penfold Pelican. The winch and the lifting tackle were small and compact, but capable of supporting a pregnant elephant, and Gretchen was obviously a competent pilot. With any luck the escape should proceed smoothly, and even if we failed to recover Calamai's treasure, I'd already been well paid for the evening's work. One thousand pounds, cash on the nail, and in advance of future remuneration.

And if we did recover the treasure those royalties would be worth a fortune. Though discredited and officially dead, Hurst-Hutchins had many friends and he'd found a potential buyer and agreed to terms. Mr Cort W. Neilsen, the American billionaire, was already on his way to London and Mr Neilsen's yacht, appropriately named the *Midas*, was anchored off Torquay. Apart from loving the sea, Mr Neilsen loved beautiful things and money meant nothing to him. Neither did morals, and providing our trade goods were genuine he was prepared to cough up like a gentleman and ask no awkward questions. The dinner service would be shipped away to a private store in Texas and that would be that. Neilsen would gloat over his purchase. We'd spend his money.

An excellent arrangement and the escape plan appeared faultless. Toylar's patients were frightened by bangs and on every Guy Fawkes Night he issued them with sleeping pills and packed them off to bed early. But one patient wouldn't swallow her pills, because Peggy had visited Normanton Towers again and Cat was briefed. Cat Guthrie would retire to her room at eight-thirty, get into bed, and turn off the lights. At nine o'clock the sleeper would awaken, put on warm garments and hammer the wedge Peg had given her under the door. At five minutes past nine she would focus her bedside lamp at the skylight and flash it on and off at three-second intervals. A signal to direct us home.

Everything had been planned to the letter and everything was going well. Even the met. forecasters were correct for once and, as they'd promised, the weather was exactly what we needed. No rain to douse the firework displays, but clouds to conceal our approach. Thick, heavy clouds, though they didn't hamper Gretchen's navigation. One of Booth's henchmen ('old Owl-Eye Osterbury; night-fighter boffin') had devised a cunning gadget which was far more effective than any radar scanner. A television camera connected to a cathode-ray tube dangled beneath the chopper and we could see and remain unseen. Owl-Eye had even provided his set with colour and the picture displayed on the screen was rather beautiful. Car lights and the lights of buildings; flashing advertising signs and the amber strings of roads and motorways; the tiny volcanoes of bonfires, and rockets hurtling into the sky. Toys to maim children, terrify animals and destroy property, and one rocket almost destroyed Owl-Eye's apparatus. It burst right beside the camera, the screen flickered wildly and for a moment I thought Gretchen would have to change to radar.

But no harm was done. The picture soon cleared and a minute or two later my pilot grunted cheerfully and swung the aircraft to port. A much bigger bonfire was in view, a really spectacular blaze with Roman candles and Catherine wheels belching around it, and a fair-sized crowd could be seen through the smoke. Normanton Village was holding its annual festival.

The Barnsby Burning is a jolly occasion these days, and I'd forgotten its grim origin till Miss Sweeting delivered a history lesson. In the year 1557, one Solomon Barnsby, rector of the parish and an overbold Protestant, penned a tract condemning Queen Mary Tudor's character and religious beliefs in no uncertain terms. 'Slave of Spain . . . Papal Spitlicker . . . Whore of the Roman Hills,' were a few of those terms and Barnsby paid dearly for them. Queen Mary wasn't called Bloody for nothing and her reaction was swift and severe. Rector Solomon Barnsby was roasted alive on his own village green.

A sad event, which somehow became associated with the Guy Fawkes tradition and is now commemorated by booze, bangs and a bombardment which was becoming severe. Two salvos of rockets overshot the camera, and when they exploded before the cockpit cowling, I saw my pilot face to face, as Tennyson's poem puts it. Gretchen Schmidt looked as calm and fearless as her famous relative probably looked during the battle for Berlin, and far more confident. Hanna Reitsch had failed to rescue Hitler because he didn't want to be rescued. Cat Guthrie was ready and waiting and Fräulein Schmidt was eager to bring her in.

'There is the signal, Herr Easter, so hook yourself on to the line and prepare to jump.' We were hovering above the asylum, and though most of the windows were in darkness, Cat's skylight was flashing away and my Luminax watch showed that our schedule was exact. Five minutes past nine and the moment of truth.

'Are you ready?' Gretchen-Hanna-Brünnhilde pressed a button and a hatch slid open to reveal the gloom below. 'Good. You have your torch and your hammer and chisel to force an entry, and the harness is secure.' She noted that all was in order and transferred her hand to the winch controls.

'Go, Herr Easter, and may God go with you.' The blessing was delivered like a battle cry, but it changed to a curse when I hesitated. 'What the hell are you waiting for? Why do you delay?'

Simple questions. The Purple Hearts were wearing off and Cat's idol had feet of clay which had started to crumble as I stared at the gaping hole.

'Jump, Herr Easter. Colonel Booth is relying on you and so are we all.' *Das Mädchen* was perplexed as well as impatient and she shook her head. 'The job is easy and foolproof, but the schedule must be observed.'

She was right on two points. The timing was important and her role was easy enough. All she had to do was to hold the chopper in position and haul us up when I jerked the line to show that Cat was strapped to the second harness. Simple routine tasks, but I had to . . .

'You have to prove that you are a man, William Easter.' Though I hadn't expressed my fears she sensed them and her voice softened. 'A man I could love, William, and I fancy you. From the moment I saw you outside the colonel's house, I knew that you were the one for me.' She switched to automatic control and frowned at me. 'You looked so strong and beautiful . . . so boyish and brave, and if you prove your bravery I shall make you a promise.' She moved across the swaying cabin towards me and I smelled perfume mingling with the rubbery tang of her flying suit.

'After our mission is completed I shall show you some tricks you don't know about.'

I'm sure that was true. But though Brünnhilde would make a change from Peg's flabby charms, I could guess what the tricks were and they didn't tempt me. I lack the masochistic urge and have no desire to be fettered or flogged or kicked around by a pair of thigh boots.

'Yes, we shall do some very interesting things together, you and

I.' She leaned forward and I thought she was going to kiss me. 'But duty comes before pleasure and Mrs Guthrie is waiting.'

I was right on both counts. Brünnhilde did kiss me and she was a sadist. Her kiss was a mere peck on my lips and it was accompanied by a blow from her fist that slammed me in the stomach and sent me reeling back.

Backward into the hatch . . . Forward into the dark.

If the nylon line hadn't been elastic, the harness would probably have crushed my ribs, and when the slack was taken up I jerked and bounced like a yo-yo on a string. An unnerving motion which seemed to continue for hours and I was still half-stunned by Brünnhilde's blow. By the time I regained my senses I was under the cloud and Normanton Towers was rushing to meet me.

The big, box-like house looked enormous and threatening in the semi-darkness. Gloom behind, and fire and flame lighting up the front. The set for a low-budget movie and I wouldn't have been surprised to see Count Dracula waiting on the roof to welcome me. I felt naked and exposed in the glare from the village green, but I blessed Solomon Barnsby's annual requiem. The patients were doped and asleep, and their attendants were probably watching the display. The bangs and whooshes and zoops provided a secure audio screen, and though Negroes are supposed to have keener ears than whites, even Dr Toylar wouldn't be able to hear the throb of the chopper.

Count Dracula was not in evidence (praise da Lawd), but my welcome continued. Cat was still flashing away to guide me in, but I didn't need guiding. Gretchen Schmidt might be a sadistic cow, but she was an expert pilot and Owl-Eye Osterbury's camera was equally efficient. The line carried me straight down to my destination and I almost forgave Brünnhilde before I landed. Almost . . . not quite.

The arrangement was that I should be deposited gently on to the flat roof, prise open the skylight and pass the second harness to Cat. Once she was securely attached, I had to signal that all was ready and we would be hauled away together.

A sound scheme, but too well executed; too accurately carried out. Brünnhilde was an expert aviator, but she lacked patience and no manufacturer of fragile goods would have employed her as a packer. She dropped me dead on target. She dropped me far too fast.

I remember bellowing shortly before my feet hit the skylight. I remember hearing the glass crunch under the impact. I remember the stab of a sliver piercing my arm. I seem to think that I bellowed again before the window rim slammed my forehead. I'm not quite sure about that, but I do remember seeing stars.

'Bill . . . Bill . . . Darling Bill.' A voice was screeching in my ear, but I tried to ignore it. I was tired and contented and I wanted to return to the heavens and sleep.

I know that seeing stars is a cliché, but I had seen them. I'd actually watched Arcturus and Orion and Venus waltzing through the purple night and they were far more beautiful than the garish fireworks banging away outside the broken skylight. I'd fought the good fight and been carried to paradise. The battle was o'er, the journey done, and I was at rest and at peace.

'Bill . . . Wake up, Bill.' The battle was not over. The words were punctuated by slaps, the screeches became frenzied and I opened my eyes reluctantly. Cat Guthrie was bent over me and she had already donned her harness and was impatient to be off. Rightly impatient, because my entry had roused Toylar and his guards and I could hear them moving in the passage. Before long they'd start to break down the door, but I wasn't going to stop them. I was too weary to lift a finger.

'Good . . . Good, Bill. That's my boy.' The slapping stopped and Cat beamed at me. 'Give the signal, darling. Tell your friends to get us out of here.'

'You tell them, Cat. Tug the rope three times and then leave me alone to die.' I fainted again, but only for a moment and when I opened my eyes a second time, I saw the order had been obeyed. Cat was suspended above me and I was being dragged after her through the skylight. Freedom lay ahead, and darkness below. The dark face of Dr Toylar who had entered the room and was watching our ascent.

Merely watching, which surprised me. I'd expected the doctor to register wrath, and demonstrate his physical powers. To leap up at my feet, to tear his woolly hair, to stamp the floor like Rumpelstiltskin in a rage. To show some sign of frustration and fury.

Cyrus Toylar's prisoner had escaped, so why did he stand there watching us so calmly? Why was he smiling?

9

'Yes – Yes – Yes. There is no doubt whatsoever. No doubt at all.' Many old people tend to repeat themselves and Mr Jonathan Haddock, senior partner of Harlow, Haddock & Clap, was very, very old. His voice quavered with age and his appearance suited his name; a dried-up body, a face as wrinkled as the skin of a smoked fish, eyes even redder than Hurst-Hutchins's. As Cat, Peggy and I were ushered into his sanctum, I thought I was looking at a revitalized Egyptian mummy.

'Yes, Mrs Guthrie, I am quite satisfied, and please forgive my rather impertinent scrutiny.' He lowered a long-range magnifying glass and clipped a *pince-nez* to his nose. 'Tom Moscow's daughter . . . Little Cathy, whom I played with when you were a child. I'm delighted to see that you are fully recovered, and you and your good fiancé and his lady sister are most welcome here.

'Please sit down and make yourselves comfortable while I contact my clerk.' He motioned us to three spartan chairs and, though they were far from comfortable, I was glad of a seat. Peggy had removed the glass splinter from my left arm and dressed the wound, but it was throbbing painfully and my head ached. My memory had been affected too when I crashed against the skylight, and Cat's escape from the asylum was as shadowy as a bad dream. I couldn't recall being hoisted back into the helicopter. I could hardly remember seeing Toylar staring up at me, but I knew I'd been wrong in thinking he smiled. Dr Cyrus Toylar had had nothing to smile about, because his guinea pig had sprouted wings and flown away. I'd mistaken a snarl of anger for a smile and Toylar was furious.

I was still slightly stunned, and I should have been in bed, but Cat had insisted that fiancé Bill and sister Peg accompanied her to Haddock's office and she'd explained why when we were alone in the lift. Cat Guthrie might be crazy, but she was no fool. She'd realized that the Booth-Hurst-Hutchins gang were crooks who'd discard her as soon as they got their hands on Moscow's letter and she wanted protection.

Cat was also ambitious and she hoped to do her benefactors in the eye. If the Calamai collection could be recovered, the proceeds wouldn't be squandered on any crackpot expedition to invade Leonia and reinstate President Hurst-Hutchins. Though the treasure might be stolen property it was Mrs Cathleen Guthrie's property. Daddy's legacy which would enable her and me and Peggy to live the life of Reilly.

A laudable ambition, but unattainable at the moment. We didn't trust our allies and the distrust was mutual. Booth's chauffeur had driven us to Haddock's place of business in the battle-scarred Humber and the colonel and Hurst-Hutchins had come along to keep us company. Lady Lesley and Gretchen and three tough male characters had followed in a Jaguar, to make assurance doubly sure. The Humber was parked in front of the building and the Jag stationed at the back. Both exits were guarded, and no act of treason was possible at the moment.

There would be a betrayal when the time was ripe, though. I've always fancied myself in the role of Judas and far more than thirty pieces of silver was at stake. Ten million U.S. dollars was the sum Mr Neilsen had agreed to pay for Calamai's gold, and I intended to collect those dollars personally.

Cat Guthrie and our other buddies could go to hell, though I wasn't going to rush matters. Till the treasure was actually located the *entente cordiale* must continue. All for each – each for all, and what a beautiful thing it is to lay down your life for a friend.

'Bring up the Moscow deed-box please, Mr Heep.' Jonathan Haddock spoke into an intercom, and I smiled because his clerk's name was as appropriate as his own. Haddock could have been born long before Victoria died. Both he and his room smacked of Dickens, so why not his staff? My numbed brain found nothing surprising at the prospect of Uriah slinking humbly into the office, but the thought amused me.

'The man's Christian name is Edward, sir.' Haddock was old and poor-sighted, but he'd noticed my amusement and grinned back; first at me and then at Cat. Peggy is virtually illiterate and she hadn't spotted the allusion.

'I'm glad that you're a Dickensian scholar and share my sense of humour, Mr Easter. I appointed Ted Heep partly on account of his nomenclature, but I can assure you that he won't defraud me. I'm a downy old bird, sir. I've got my wits about me.

'What's that?' I'd merely said that I could see he was as bright as brass, but the politeness raised a puzzled frown. Mr Haddock might have his wits, but he'd lost his faculties and he fiddled with the microphone of an antiquated hearing-aid pinned to his jacket.

'Ah, thank you, my boy.' I'd repeated the compliment more clearly and received three in return. 'Cathleen has made a fortunate choice and you are blessed with civility, charm and education.' Though his tone was friendly there was a hint of mockery in the faded red eyes, and I began to dislike Mr Jonathan Haddock. Dislike him and suspect him. It was quite possible that he had opened Moscow's sealed letter and acted accordingly. If that was true we could say farewell to any treasure. Guido Calamai's creations would have been sold long ago to swell the old villain's coffers.

'Yes, I approve of your choice, Cathleen, and I have no doubt that he'll make you a dutiful husband.' He beamed at Cat and then reread the note she'd brought with her. Another of Miss Sweeting's skilled forgeries on a sheet of headed stationery Booth had pocketed when he visited Normanton Towers. Between the heading and four imposing signatures was a typed 'To whom it may concern' certificate. Dr Cyrus Toylar and other experts had examined Mrs Cathleen Guthrie and pronounced her free of disease: mental, physical or transmittable.

'Excellent news, and I can't say how delighted I am by your recovery.' There was a loud creak as Haddock leaned back in his chair, but I didn't know whether the sound was produced by timber or arthritis. 'You are completely recovered and able to lead a happy, normal life with the lover of your choice.

'Delighted on your account and relieved on my own.' A set of dentures flashed his delight. 'I was one of your father's closest friends, but there was no denying that he was a difficult client before . . .' Haddock had been about to say, *before he went off his rocker*, or words to that effect, but he paused and rephrased the statement. '. . . before ill-health struck him.

'That sealed envelope he deposited here on the day of his demise has been a hard trust to bear, and after the three-year period ended, I was almost tempted to open it. Sir Thomas's covering note was strangely worded and I began to suspect that the envelope might contain something of a criminal nature.

'However, I resisted temptation, and I also resisted blandishments. As I've told you, I'm a downy old bird, Mr Easter.' He tapped his skull to signify that there were a few brains inside it. 'Only last week a young woman came here with a letter signed by Mrs Guthrie and requested that I should hand over the document to her. I can't remember what your friend's name was, but I sent her away with a flea in her ear, Cathleen.' Haddock's memory was as bad as mine, but in spite of his reference to age I knew who the young woman was. Though Janet Sweeting would never see fifty again, Jonathan Haddock was so old that anyone under seventy appeared youthful to him.

'Sir Thomas's instructions were adamant. The envelope was to be given to Cathleen when she claimed it in person and showed me a certificate of good health. In the event of your death, Cathleen, I or my successors were to destroy the communication with its seals intact.

'Fortunately you are alive and well and all your father's conditions have been fulfilled.' There was a tap on the door, but he paused before responding to it. 'I shall be interested to know what Thomas Moscow left you, my dear.' He looked at the door and his old voice croaked loudly. 'Come in, Mr Heep.'

Haddock's clerk may have resembled his fictional namesake, but I hardly noticed his appearance. I scarcely noticed the paper in his hand, because he was not alone and my own hand started to slide towards the flick-knife in my hip pocket.

Only started to slide, because the odds were too great. The

'I shall do what I can for you, and I don't think we need take up any more of Mr Haddock's time.' His female assistant replaced the handcuffs in a shoulder bag and Bowden relaxed and told Haddock that he would call back for an official statement at the old fool's convenience. We were preparing to leave when Toylar led the ace I'd been expecting.

'There is just one small point, Mr Haddock.' The doctor's tone had changed again and he eyed Cat sympathetically. 'Mrs Guthrie made her ill-advised escape attempt because she is desperate to know what her father's communication was. In the interest of charity would you waive legality and let her have it?'

'A difficult request, Doctor.' Haddock's bleary eyes flicked from the envelope in Heep's hand to Cat's face, and I've never seen a more woe-begone face. I've never seen a person age in minutes, and Cat Guthrie had aged. She looked almost as old as Haddock and her body had shrunk. She was frightened and defenceless and as pathetic as a half-drowned kitten. 'Extremely difficult because Sir Thomas's instructions were quite adamant, but under the circumstances I suppose . . .' Haddock hesitated, though not for long. As he'd said, the letter was a troublesome burden which he wanted to discard and he growled an order. 'Give it to her, Heep.'

'Thank you, sir.' Cat took the envelope, but there was no gratitude in her voice and no youth in her step as the inspector motioned us to the door. An old, shrunken woman left Haddock's office with a shrunken man in front of her; a man called William Easter. Though I rarely suffer from guilt I was racked by remorse as I walked away with Peggy at my heels. Cat had dreamed of love and wealth and freedom and she was going back to an asylum. Peggy and I were going to prison. We were all going down and down we went.

Down in a lift . . . down into the sunlight . . . down a flight of steps to the street. Down a slope past Booth's Humber and I saw that Bowden was right and there was no help from that quarter. Colonel Jack had fought Germans and Italians, but he wouldn't tackle the British police, and neither would I. There was a black mini bus parked behind the Humber with a constable at the wheel and our allies realized that the show was over when they saw us move towards it. Booth and the chauffeur looked away hurriedly and Hurst-Hutchins almost doubled up in consternation.

I didn't blame them. I know what happens to fools who attack rozzers, and though Toylar's gun was in his jacket and there was a tube station across the road, I never considered trying to belt him and Bowden and make a run for it. I never thought of using the flick-knife and I didn't feel it slide out of my pocket. I'd given up hope when the assault came.

'I'll take charge of that, Cathleen.' We had climbed into the bus and Toylar nodded at the envelope. Though the roof made him stoop he towered over Cat's frail, defeated body and she seemed to shrink before him. 'Give it to me immediately, girl.'

'Of course, Doctor.' She held out the package in her left hand, and as he reached for it her legs seemed to buckle and she toppled forward with a whimper.

That whimper was the first of several noises and I can still hear them clearly. The rip of paper as the envelope was torn apart. An agonized bellow as Cat's right hand shot out and the knife stabbed Toylar in the place where I'd intended to kick him. The crash as Toylar reeled sideways across a seat and the rap of his pistol falling on to the floor. Cat's triumphant giggle when she stood up . . . Bowden's gasp.

It was the inspector's turn to stare at a Lüger, but his view was brief and the final sounds were simultaneous. The pop of the silencer and the crunch of metal against bone. Cat was an expert shot and Bowden died with a third eye to guide him to eternity. A scarlet bullet hole in the exact centre of his forehead.

10

'Aren't I clever, Bill? Wasn't it a lovely piece of acting, Margaret? Have either of you seen better shooting?' Cat screeched with delight, but there was no need for her to lower her voice. We'd reached the tube station, but just missed a train and the platform was deserted. 'Bang . . . right through the middle of his skull.

'Won't you congratulate me, darling?' She put her face up to be kissed but I drew back in disgust. I'd rather have had my lips nibbled by a plague rat and I felt like taking Mrs Cathleen Guthrie by the shoulder and throwing her on to the live rail.

'Oh, you are unkind and ungrateful, Bill.' Her legs had dragged like a drunk's when we left Haddock's office, but there was nothing wrong with them now and she stamped the platform petulantly. 'What's the matter with you both? I got you away from those devils. We're safe and free and soon we'll be rich. Nobody will dare to follow us. Not while I have this.' She swung her handbag against my thigh and I felt the weight of the Lüger inside it.

'They will follow us, you little fool.' Peg spoke with an ear cocked along the platform and I knew what she was listening for. Either the rumble of a train which might give us a few hours' respite, or a police loudhailer announcing that we were trapped and had better surrender before they loosed off the tear gas or sent the dogs in. 'You killed one of their men, and they never forgive that. Even if we manage to leave this station, it'll do us no good. They'll hound us down in time and set us up for murder.'

'Hound us *down* – Set us *up*.' Cat found the phrases amusing. 'Yes I did kill one man didn't I? George Bowden has a hole in his head, and Toylar won't be thinking about women for a while.

'How he yelped when the knife caught him.' Cat's eyes twinkled at the pleasurable memory, and then she frowned at our expressions. 'But what about the others? Why did you stop me killing them? Why does everybody humiliate and frustrate me?'

'They were coppers, my dear.' I braced myself to grab the handbag. Cat was a homicidal maniac and if we could turn her in Peg and I might receive light sentences. The survivors should certainly say a kind word for us, because we'd saved their lives. Cat had been about to put Toylar out of his misery with a second bullet when I jostled her over Bowden's corpse, but she'd held on to the pistol. The driver and the policewoman would have shared their superior's fate if Peggy hadn't stationed herself in front of them as a screen till I persuaded the executioner to see reason.

Persuasion which took some time, and reason hadn't lasted long. After crossing the street, Cat's blood lust returned and she tried to run back to the bus and complete the carnage. It took our joint efforts to drag her into the station. Fortunately the blackamoors on duty were half-asleep and they didn't give us a glance.

'Coppers, Bill!' She gasped at me in genuine surprise. 'You honestly think that I killed a policeman? You don't realize who George Bowden was?' Her feet stamped again, but not in anger. They performed an ungainly tripping dance on the concrete and she burst into song.

'"Three blind mice. See how they run."' Cat Guthrie was in her late twenties, but she sang as excitedly as a toddler at a Christmas party. '"They all ran after the farmer's wife. She cut off their tails with a carving knife. Did ever you see such a thing in your life, as three blind mice?"' The singing stopped and was replaced by an insane giggle and a question.

'I wonder if your knife cut off Toylar's tail, Bill. I hope so, but don't be annoyed because I left it sticking in him.

'A nice little knife, but though I'm sorry you've lost it, I'll buy you a much better one when we've found Daddy's legacy. An inlaid blade with a blood channel . . . an ivory handle studded with pearls or rubies. You name what you want and I'll buy it for you, darling.'

'We won't find any legacy, Cat, and they don't allow convicts to carry knives.' I was about to reach for the bag, but turned round because we were no longer alone. Two shabby characters in duffle coats had walked on to the platform, and though they didn't look like rozzers, I feared the worst. Ten minutes had passed since we'd left the bus and the hunters must have followed our trail. 'You murdered a police inspector, and that puts paid to everything.'

'You and Margaret still think that George Bowden was a policeman, Bill?' She reddened with anger and glared at Peggy. 'If you can believe that you must be mad. As mad as Toylar said I was. Mad and useless and I don't need your help.' Her hand slid into the bag to bring out the pistol. 'I'll find Daddy's treasure myself and the pair of you can go to hell unless you listen to me.

'Yes, listen, Bill. Listen carefully and I'll tell you who George Bowden was.' She started to do so and before she finished my hair stood on end, though not from fear or disgust. My fears had dwindled and wind stirred my hair. The air pressure of an approaching train that would carry us away to liberty and fortune.

Cat Guthrie was a vicious cat, but she wasn't a fool, and when the train ground to a halt, I realized just how clever her performance had been.

Inspector Bowden had been Toylar's head nurse and chief strong-arm man. The policewoman was Toylar's matron. The driver of the police van was Toylar's chauffeur. Their uniforms had been borrowed from the Normanton Thespians, the asylum's amateur dramatic group, directed and produced by Dr Toylar.

Dr Cyrus Toylar had had a formidable team at his disposal, and so had Booth and Hurst-Hutchins. One certified maniac had got the better of them all.

'Of course I couldn't tell that solicitor they were impostors, Bill. He'd never have believed me, and even you and Margaret would have thought I was lying.' We had left the train five stations down the line and Cat was continuing her explanation in a quiet public house. 'I knew that the only way was to pretend I was hypnotized by Toylar and get the gun from him.

'And Toylar should be back at the Towers now.' She looked at the bar clock and tittered. 'If Matron's started to stitch him up, I hope she's run out of anaesthetic. I hope the bastard's screaming while we're sitting laughing at him and enjoying ourselves in comfort.

'Cheers, partners.' She raised a glass of orange juice. Toylar's patients were kept on the wagon and Cat had lost her fondness for alcohol. 'Here's to us.'

'Cheers.' Peg responded to the toast and I followed suit, but I didn't feel cheerful or comfortable and I wasn't enjoying myself, though things were going our way.

Cat was probably correct in saying that Toylar had returned to the asylum and he and his assistants wouldn't report Bowden's death to the authorities. Mr Bogus Inspector Bowden would be discreetly buried in the garden.

Old Haddock and his clerk would present no problems either. They'd probably receive a telephone call stating that the public prosecutor had decided to drop charges against us because the publicity might endanger Cat's health.

The Booth faction had probably decided to accept defeat.

They'd certainly been too stunned to follow us to the tube.

We probably had nothing to fear from the law.

A lot of probables, but Cat's ruse had worked exactly as she hoped it would work, and there'd been only one flaw in the performance. She couldn't control herself. If Peggy and I hadn't intervened the real police would be examining a mini-bus containing four corpses and they'd soon discover whom the corpses had belonged to and start asking questions.

Cat Guthrie was too clever. As clever as Hitler and Stalin, and like those gentry she was unpredictable and dangerous. I admired her, I respected her and I was grateful to her.

It was an excellent idea to cut out Hurst-Hutchins and the Booths and grab the treasure for ourselves and I was bursting with enthusiasm for clever Mrs Guthrie. But I was also scared of her and had come to a decision. As soon as she led us to that treasure, Mrs Guthrie must die.

'Now let's see what Daddy says.' Cat had regained a trace of sanity and though the bar was almost empty, she glanced cautiously around before unzipping her handbag. 'What did he leave me? Where did he hide my legacy . . . my treasure.

'No . . . no . . . no.' Sanity vanished after she opened the bag and I sympathized with her cries of frustration. I'd forgotten that Toylar had been clutching the envelope before she stabbed him, and half of it had remained in his grasp. All Cat had to show was a torn fragment of paper with a signature and a postscript.

'My mind and memory are faulty and I may be wrong regarding the Geneva account number.' Moscow's handwriting was also faulty, and when I took the fragment from Cat I could hardly decipher the spidery print.

'If I am wrong, the bank will refuse your request, but the Irishman might still be alive, so go to Essex first.' The message ended with five words which told me nothing. The name of a dead politician; the title of a best-selling novel.

'Timothy Michael Healy . . . Animal Farm.'

11

'Yes, I knew your father, Missus; more's the pity.' Mr Timothy Healy wasn't a politician and he hadn't died. We'd located him through an Essex telephone directory and hired a car to take us to his place of business. I'd much rather have been interviewed by a well-groomed Swiss bank manager, because the business stank and so did its owner. They reeked of dung and musk and urine and I kept pulling at a cigarette in vain attempts to stifle nausea.

TIM HEALY'S ANIMAL RESCUE CENTRE was a dilapidated barn surrounded by muddy pens. Mr Healy's cages looked as though they'd never been cleaned out, and their occupants were dejected and uncared for and half-starved. Some of them were crippled and diseased and Healy shared their infirmities. His body was bent like a hoop, his face was pitted with the scars of old pustules and there wasn't a hair on his scaly head. I'd hated him from the moment he came hobbling across the field to open a gate for us.

'Aye, more's the pity, though I bear Sir Thomas no ill feelings. He paid for his foolishness. We all paid, and I'm still paying.' He cleared his throat and spat out a gob of yellow phlegm that landed between my feet.

'Watch yerself, sir.' I had drawn back and he motioned me to keep away from the mangy chimpanzee tethered to the wall by a leather collar and an iron chain. 'That fella's a real killer. I got him from a circus because he tried to strangle the trainer.

'Powerdrive Pete was his name then, but Peter Pest's what I call him now.' Healy spat again and his phlegm dribbled down the animal's face. 'Not a bad name either, because Pest is what the devil's going to get in the near future. I've sold him to a government research establishment and they'll pump a dose of mutated *bacillus pestis* into his veins.' He glowered at the chimp, which was whimpering as though it already knew what the future held. 'Yes, a shot of bubonic plague will teach you manners, Peter. They all learn manners after the hypodermics dig into 'em.' He grinned at my expression and nodded around his misery farm.

'I gather that you disapprove of my work, sir. A lot of people do, but they're fools, and I regard myself as a public benefactor. I collect strays and other unwanted brutes and they go to hospitals and laboratories all over the country. Where would science be without me? Where would you be, Miss Moscow?

'Sorry, it's Mrs Guthrie now. You told me that on the telephone but I keep forgetting things.' He scratched his forehead with a blackened fingernail. 'Me brain's as bad as me body, and though Dr Toylar promised I'd get no worse, I'll get no better.

'But you're healthy enough, Missus?' He squinted at Cat as though examining a possible purchase. 'Did your father fail to infect you, or has Toylar found a cure for that Italian's disease?

'Oh yes, Sir Thomas said he'd pass on his illness to you, though don't ask me why. Maybe Satan whispered a word in his ear.' Healy's facial muscles were paralysed, but though he couldn't smile, he could laugh and his laughter was a chilling sound. As chilling as the mind of Thomas Moscow.

'I was ill, Mr Healy.' The news that she might have been deliberately infected hadn't distressed Cat and she spoke quite calmly. 'I am now completely cured, however, and I think my father gave you something to keep for me.'

'That's true, Missus, but I can't remember what the thing was.' He looked away from us and shook his horrible, wizened head. 'Sir Thomas said that you might pay me a visit one day, but I don't recall his actual words. Did he want me to tell you about them, Mrs Guthrie? Do you share his interest in the sewers?'

He pointed towards a wire-fronted crate at the back of the barn and my nausea increased. The box was crammed with huge, brown sewer-rats which were almost as repellent as their owner. 'I loathe them bastards, Missus. I hate 'em as though they were human beings who'd done me an injury on purpose, and maybe they did.

'Clever rats are . . . much, much cleverer than all the other bleeders put together.' He spat at the chimp a second time and grimaced at the rest of his menagerie; cats and dogs and guinea pigs, a rhesus monkey, two puma kittens and a wretched creature which might have been a lion cub.

'Yes, rats are clever and cunning. Dead cunning, and that's why your father's dead, Missus. That's why I look like this.

'And what was it that Sir Thomas told me to keep for you?' He paused and scratched his skull again. 'No, I can't remember and it all happened a long time ago. Must be nine years since your Dad first approached me. Six years before we realized what was happening to us. Nearly four years when Moscow came back and said they'd decided to kill themselves.

'He did give me something though; something which you had to collect in person. Let's go and have a look in the office, and while we're looking, I'll tell you about our little experiment that went wrong.

'Aye, nine years ago, and there were five of them.' He muttered to himself and led the way to a door beside the rat cage. 'Moscow and Toylar, Rolfe and Blake and the woman. What was her name? Something like Holden or Heldon.

'No, I can't recall her name, but I'll never forget her screams.' His eyes were fixed on the rats as he turned the doorknob. 'How that woman screamed when the bastards leapt at her.'

Healy's office was as foul as the rest of his premises, but I ceased to notice the squalor after he'd started to tell the story. Though he rambled at times and kept breaking off to rummage through piles of dusty papers, he held my full attention from beginning to end.

Sir Thomas Moscow had spotted Calamai's Borgia ring device in the Cyclops goblet and shown his findings to a group of friends. Toylar and another doctor called Blake, a physicist named Rolfe and the woman whose name Healy couldn't remember, though I guessed it was Hilda Helmer. They were all very interested when analysis showed that the poison was biological; razor-sharp spores which could lie dormant for centuries till moisture revived them.

'Wine, water and blood, Mrs Guthrie.' Healy chuckled while he unlocked a roll-top desk. 'Your father was a religious man and he liked to think that the elements of the mass changed the nature of his demons. A mere fancy, of course. Any non-toxic liquid would activate the spores, though blood was needed for them to grow and reproduce themselves. Human blood or animal blood, and I'd got plenty of animals.

'But why . . . why . . . why did they come to me?' Healy's chuckle changed to a sigh, but his question was addressed to Fate and the answer was obvious. Moscow and his colleagues had located an original Renaissance poison; a subject which has stimulated scores of historical novelists. They wanted to find out exactly what that poison could do, and they intended to announce their discovery dramatically. No garrulous lab assistants were going to discuss their work over beer mugs or coffee cups, and they didn't need any assistance. Tim Healy had all they wanted: animals.

Toylar and Blake produced cultures from the spore tissues, victims were infected and the results proved satisfactory. The experimenters were delighted by the fruits of their labours, and one interesting point was soon apparent. The disease was governed by the size and life-cycle of the host. Dogs and monkeys showed no sign of distress till the joke ended and Healy incinerated them. Rats responded within a month.

Mental disturbance was the first symptom. The creatures became abnormally ferocious and had to be housed in separate compartments; physical changes soon followed. Healy described the aberrations in vivid detail which I won't repeat, but they pleased Moscow and his pals. Sir Thomas paid daily visits to the hell shop and he positively chortled over his victims. Sir Thomas intended to write a thesis on Calamai's poison and hoped it would get him elected to the Royal Society.

But Moscow's visits were made during the day and it was during a dark night that pain and ferocity were joined by cunning. Some of the animals stopped tearing at the steel wire of their cages and started work on the door hinges, which were brass. They had gnawed through them when dawn broke.

The dark night was followed by a clear, bright morning. The first Sunday morning in the merrie month of May and, with the exception of Toylar, all the team drove out to Essex to view their progress. Healy was suffering from a hangover, but his visitors were in fine fettle. Moscow fresh from a mass at Saint Egbert's, the doctor and the physicist looking forward to a round of golf after the examination, Hilda Helmer as gay as a cricket.

A gaiety which vanished after Healy led them into the barn, and as he'd said, how that woman screamed. I bet she did, but I had no sympathy for Miss Helmer. My sympathies were with the rats.

. . . . .

'You can imagine what it was like.' Healy was reliving the incident and sweat dribbled from his face and sprinkled the papers on the desk. 'We suspected nothing till we saw the open cages and then they flew at us like darts. One of the devils had its teeth in my wrist before I slammed him against the wall, and though only a few of them were free, we was all torn and bleeding by the time Sir Thomas killed the last bastard with his walking stick.

'Can you picture what we felt, sir?

'Pain, disgust and terror.' He had appealed to me and I didn't need much imagination to appreciate his feelings.

'But what happened afterwards, Mr Healy? When did you begin to feel ill?'

'Not for a long time. We slaughtered the rest of the rats, and the monkeys as well, and then drove straight off to Toylar's place. He gave us shots of penicillin and suchlike and said we should be O.K.' Healy looked at a photograph he had found in one of the desk drawers. 'I thought I was O.K. too. We all did till I started to have them headaches and nightmares.

'Horrible dreams they was and me temper got bad. I went on the booze and picked fights deliberately. Every pub in the neighbourhood had banned me before I guessed something was wrong and decided to go and see Toylar.' He held out the photograph, but it meant nothing to us and we'd never seen the sitter. A tall man in his twenties with fair hair and rather handsome features.

'Toylar took a sample of me blood and then he phoned Moscow and the others and said they'd better come over at the double. When they got there he made some more tests and gave us the verdict.

'We'd all been infected by those rats, but I was the lucky one.

I might recover, but the rest hadn't a chance in hell, unless Toylar came up with a cure before the bugs really got to work on 'em.

'Lucky! Yes, Toylar called me lucky, but what's your opinion, Mrs Guthrie?' Healy was still holding out the picture and he nodded as Cat winced. 'Yes, that's what I looked like four years ago. You didn't recognize me, did you? But at least I'm alive and I suppose one can count that a blessing. I survived because I'd been bitten by the first rat they poisoned and the disease progressed so rapidly in my system that it outgrew its strength and some bugs of me own started a counter-attack. Toylar spouted a lot of technical jargon which I didn't understand and I didn't try to. I just lay on his hospital bed and moaned.'

'I understand, Mr Healy.' Peg spoke smugly. Though she had no academic qualifications, she shared Cat's hypochondria and spent long hours browsing through textbooks in the public libraries. 'Because the micro-organism was approaching its terminal stage when the rat bit you, your own defence mechanisms were alerted in time and . . .'

'In time, you say.' Peg had hoped to deliver a pompous lecture on bacteriology, but Healy cut her short. 'If you had a scrap of charity in your fat body you'd not speak like that. I was in such agony that Toylar had to strap me to the bed before the germs started to die, and when I saw me face in the mirror I wished I'd died with 'em.

'I still wish I was dead sometimes, Mrs Guthrie; as dead as your dad and the others.' He pushed the photograph away and opened a second drawer. 'Yes they all took the easy way home. Gas and fire killed Sir Thomas. Rolfe and Blake chucked 'emselves off a yacht in the Irish Sea, the woman . . .

'No, I can't remember how she went, but she's dead all right, though they never found her body.' Healy was speaking to himself again while he rummaged through the drawer. 'Moscow told me they'd decided to commit suicide when he came back here for the last time.

'Yes, he came back and me memory's coming back. I can see him and hear him as though he was with us now. Very tall and grim he looked, and I was right scared when he made me swear an oath to keep this for you.' Healy had found what he was looking for and he took a plastic cylinder from the drawer. 'Your property, Mrs Guthrie, but there are some conditions to be observed before I hand it over, and there's not enough light to read them here.' He squinted at a sheet of paper which had been attached to the roll with a rubber band. 'Let's go outside and see what your dad wanted.'

He led the way out of the gloomy room with Cat following him and, as she passed me, my own memory started to return and I recalled something Cyrus Toylar had said during our first visit to Normanton Towers, something which troubled me while we walked between the stinking cages and their wretched occupants.

Toylar had failed to cure Cat, but he'd found that certain drugs could slow down her condition, and it might be some time before any physical symptoms appeared. Was it possible that the disease would accelerate if she was deprived of those drugs? That it had already accelerated?

No, the possibility was too disturbing to think about, and I tried to reassure myself when Healy halted in a patch of sunlight near the chained chimpanzee. The gloom and the stench had affected my eyes and they were deceiving me. Cat was sweating as badly as Healy and the blisters on her forehead were drops of moisture. A gumboil must be causing the swelling on her cheek, and she'd brushed against a patch of cobwebs. Yes, cobwebs accounted for the grey streaks in her hair.

'That's better.' Healy was examining the note. 'Your dad's writing is a bit cramped, but his instructions are clear enough. Before I give you the package I need three things in return.' He was so intent on the conditions that he never noticed Cat open her bag and take out the Lüger. Neither did I, because I was watching her face and it wouldn't have made any difference if I had seen the pistol. All human life is expendable and Tim Healy's life was worthless. I wouldn't have raised a finger to save him.

'Proof of identity, Mrs Guthrie. A health certificate signed by Toylar and two other recognized medical authorities.

'Most important of all, a . . .' Healy cleared his throat to spit again before stating Moscow's final requirement, but the sputum never left his lips and we didn't hear what the requirement was. Cat's aim was as accurate as ever and he dropped the cylinder and fell back with the letter clenched in his hand. I imagine he was dead when his body hit the barn floor.

The floor was damp and greasy, and that was Cat's undoing. Her feet slipped, the bullet's recoil sent her spinning against the chimpanzee, and Healy hadn't lied about the animal's character. Powerdrive Pete (a much nicer name than Peter Pest) was equally vicious. He'd almost tugged Cat's head from her shoulders when I saw her eyes glaze and she went to join Daddy Moscow.

12

We'd had no time to restrain Powerdrive Pete, and no reason to do so. I'd already decided that Cat would have to die and the chimp had saved me the trouble of killing her. Nor was there time to examine Cat's face to see if I was right about the disease symptoms, or prise the letter from Healy's rigid grasp. Pete's blow for freedom had excited the other animals and their frenzied barks and snarls and gibberings might have brought unwelcome visitors to the scene. Peggy picked up the plastic cylinder, which was the thing we wanted, and we hurried to the car, leaving the pistol behind.

The plastic was tough and securely sealed and the only tools supplied by the car renter were a jack and a wheel brace. Peggy broke a fingernail before she gave up trying to open the package by hand, and I stopped in a village and told her to buy a Stanley knife. While she looked for a shop, I went to a telephone kiosk and kept a mental promise I'd made when we first entered Mr Healy's animal Belsen. An R.S.P.C.A. official was grateful for my information and assured me that one of his inspectors would visit the establishment within an hour. I hoped that the inspector had strong nerves, because he'd be in for quite a shock when he saw Cat and Healy.

But that was his misfortune not mine, and I considered our situation after I rang off and walked back to the car park. Police enquiries didn't worry me, because there was nothing to connect us with Cat. She and Peggy had remained in the pub while I went to hire the car, and though the police would discover that Cat had escaped from Normanton Towers, Toylar couldn't inform on us without incriminating himself.

Nor was I worried about retribution from Booth and his army of fanatics. With any luck Peggy and I would be far away from England-Home-and-Beauty before they got wind of us, and I'd have hired enough thugs of my own to send 'em packing.

The fact that Moscow had lodged a second document in a Geneva bank didn't bother me either. Toylar might have the account number but he hadn't got Cat, and Moscow would have left orders that it could only be collected by her in person. If Cyrus Toylar tried to fool a hard-headed Swiss banker he'd have to take an expert actress along with him.

No problems from the law, and no problems from Toylar or our former buddies. Our only problems were to find the treasure and dispose of it, and I was confident that the cylinder contained an answer to the first question. Detailed instructions pin-pointing Moscow's hiding place and telling us how to enter it.

Everything was going smoothly and I was so elated that I hummed 'Land of Hope and Glory' as I approached the car. But the humming stopped abruptly when I climbed in and saw Peg's expression.

'Nothing, Bill. Nothing that makes sense.' She had cut open the plastic roll and found its contents disappointing. 'We can forget about the treasure and we've risked our lives for nothing. Moscow was potty and this is all he left his daughter.' Peggy was quivering with frustration and I didn't know whether she was about to burst into tears or hit me. 'See for yourself, Smart Alec Easter.' She brandished a sheet of paper in my face. 'Just an amateurish, childish, obscene doodle, and a lot of scribbles that are Greek to me.'

'They *are* Greek, Peggy.' I took the paper from her and, after a moment my good humour returned. Though I was booted out of university before receiving a degree, I can read Greek and I was starting to read Moscow's mind.

'Obscene – yes. Potty – perhaps. Childish – most definitely not. Cat Guthrie had had an expensive education and Tom Moscow was a classical scholar. Moscow also had a suspicious nature and he wrote in Greek for security's sake. If Healy had decided to break his vow and open the cylinder, this would have made him none the wiser.' I smiled at the drawing at the top of the page and paraphrased the lines of sloping writing for Peggy's benefit.

'Moscow starts by reminding Cat that the letter she must have received from Haddock told her to visit a place called the House of Stethno, but it is essential that she should obtain these instructions first and observe them to the letter.

'The House of Stethno; another precaution in case old Haddock proved untrustworthy. He probably knows Greek, but the name wouldn't have told him much, as it's in dialect.

'I'll try to translate Moscow's instructions as well as I can, though his writing is a bit difficult here and there.' That was putting it mildly. Many of the words were almost indecipherable, and Moscow had fancied himself as a poet and delivered the information in verse.

> My guardian sits above the fire,
> Watching my gold and nursing her ire.
> Gold that is waiting behind the grate,
> Screened by Stethno's murderous hate.

Doggerel, but it contained a cunningly coded message which would be meaningless to anyone who wasn't in the know, and the second stanza stressed that Moscow's murderous guardian had to be treated with proper respect. His final lines told me how to treat her.

> Press the eyes which turn flesh to stone,
> Twist the snakes in the metal bone.
> Follow the sequence from left to right,
> The song of the black and white bird in flight.

A fair rendering of the jingle, though I say so myself, but Peggy was not impressed, and the drawing still conveyed nothing to her. Why should it have done? Peg had never seen the original, and as she had said, Moscow's reproduction was an amateurish doodle.

But I knew who'd sat for that drawing and the knowledge made me climb out of the car and hurry back to the phone box, though there was no need for haste. The guardian couldn't leave her post, because she was riveted to it.

Stethno was sitting on the treasure . . . on *our* treasure.

'Hold the line please . . . Hang on please . . . Wait a moment please.' I'd got through to a London hotel, but the person I wanted to talk to was difficult to contact. The switchboard girl put me through to his suite reluctantly. A female secretary demanded my business and sounded contemptuous when I said it was private and personal. I thought I'd been cut off when a male voice took over and asked me to spell out my name as his colleague hadn't quite caught it.

'Signor Guido Andrea C-A-L-A-M-A-I. One second please.' He'd repeated the letters aloud, and the time limit was exactly one second. The instrument had been snatched from his hand and I heard the great man himself.

'Is that you, Bishop Hurst-Hutchins?'

'It is not, Mr Neilsen, and you can forget about the bishop.' Cort W. Neilsen was blessed with a warm, friendly drawl, but I replied coldly. Warmth and friendship hadn't made him a multi-millionaire; Mr Neilsen was a hard citizen who'd fought his way from the bottom to the top and he owned things. A hell of a lot of things. Half a dozen newspapers and a couple of airlines. A brewery which manufactured inferior lager made from potato peelings, and a chain of supermarkets. A film company, the controlling interest in a merchant bank, a few hundred petrol stations and . . . You name the pies and C.W.N. probably had a finger in them.

Neilsen's business empire was far flung, and so was his personal empire. Yachts and villas and penthouses, executive jets and race-horses and a heavyweight boxer. He was also a philanthropist who spent large sums fostering young artists, and a connoisseur who hoarded the works of the old. Mr Neilsen's private gallery was one of the finest in the world and his taste was impeccable. Rubens and Rembrandt and Leonardo, Goya and Michelangelo and Cellini were all represented. C.W.N. had the magpie bug and he bought the best.

But to date he hadn't been able to buy a Calamai and he wanted to. He wanted a Calamai very badly, which was why Gerry Hurst-Hutchins had approached him, and why he'd come rushing to London. I'd got the whip hand over C. W. Neilsen, and I adopted the tone of one sharp dealer addressing another.

'Bishop Hurst-Hutchins is out of the running, Mr Neilsen. He's a back number and you'll get nothing from him. I'm in the chair now so if you hope to buy the Calamai dinner service, you'll have to talk turkey and play ball with me.'

'What a lot of metaphors you use, sir.' Neilsen's laugh was as warm as his voice, but I could sense that Gerry's failure had frustrated him. 'No criticism intended, however, and may I reply in a similar vein. I don't give a fart whom I deal with, and I'd sacrifice my left bollock to get hold of those Calamai pieces.

'The back-numbered bishop, as you describe him, promised that he could deliver the goods and I'm waiting to take delivery. The payment I promised Hurst-Hutchins is also waiting at my London bank. Dollar bearer bonds, which can be cashed anywhere in the western world.

'I'm ready to fulfil my side of the bargain, so will you state your position, Signor Anonymous, or whatever you like to call yourself?' Though he laughed again his frustration was even more apparent, and in spite of his wealth and his power, I almost felt sorry for Cort W. Neilsen. Like Sir Thomas Moscow he had become obsessed by Guido Calamai, and he really might be prepared to trade half his virility for a dream.

A sacrifice which didn't impress me. I had no interest in his testicles. I only wanted his money, but I knew the kind of man he was. Mr Neilsen lusted after Calamai's dinner service. He longed to fondle it and stroke it, and gloat over his stolen toys in some secret vault. He was a fanatic who would do almost anything to achieve his end and his next questions were hissed through the phone. 'When can I take delivery, sir, and how can I trust you?'

I outlined the situation and his frustration vanished. He sounded as pally as a politician on polling day. 'Fair enough, but let me recap what you've said. You have proof that Sir Thomas Moscow substituted the Calamai treasure with fakes, and you know where the original pieces are hidden.

'But you are reluctant to lead me to the hiding place without a down payment and I don't blame you. Whatever people say, there's no honour amongst thieves, and I might decide to betray you as you've betrayed Bishop Hurst-Hutchins.' There was a third attractive laugh, though I didn't much care for the word *betray*. I hadn't betrayed Gerry Hurst-Hutchins. I'd left him cowering in a bulletproof car, too terrified to follow me.

'Your suggestion is that you produce two pieces of the dinner service, and provided my experts certify that they are genuine, I will hand over a quarter of the bonds to one of your accomplices. We shall then visit Moscow's hiding-place together and you will receive the rest of the sum I promised Hurst-Hutchins. That will complete your side of the bargain. Transport and other technicalities must be my responsibility.

'Yes, a reasonable proposition, sir, so when and where can you deliver the samples?' He waited patiently while I made a calculation and stuffed more money into the phone meter. Peggy and I had a long journey ahead of us and we might run into difficulties before Moscow's guardian was placated. Nor did I fancy a journey back with the samples on board. The police often search cars for I.R.A. bombs and they'd be equally interested to find a pair of *objets d'art* in the boot.

'Bonnie Scotland, eh.' The rendezvous seemed to please him. 'You want me to go to the Alexandra Hotel in Oban, and you will contact me there during the next three days.

'That is quite satisfactory, though there is one minor point I would like to change, if you have no objection.' Mr Neilsen was an adaptable man. His tone was apologetic and the point really was minor. 'Though the Alex is an excellent establishment, I'd rather stay at the Duke of Abervann. A personal preference, because I recently purchased the Duke, and it would be an opportunity for me to sample its service as well as your wares, sir.'

I had no objection to the Duke, and we finished our conversation on the best of terms and said how much we looked forward to a face-to-face meeting.

A nice man, Mr Neilsen; as nice a man as I'd had the pleasure of doing business with, and where business was concerned I trusted him financially. But I didn't trust him emotionally, and though he'd tried to appear nonchalant about Hurst-Hutchins's failure, the act hadn't fooled me. He was desperate to get his clutches on the Calamai treasure, and provided the goods were delivered, I'd have made a friend for life. If they weren't delivered I'd have made a powerful enemy and I rang off without giving him any name.

A worthless piece of secrecy, because Hurst-Hutchins must have informed Neilsen about the betrayal already and told him who the betrayer was. Information which wouldn't bother Mr Neilsen. All he wanted was that dinner service and he couldn't care less whom he got it from. If he didn't get it . . . God help me and Peggy.

In spite of his pleasant manners, Mr Cort Wilhelm Neilsen lacked the qualities of mercy and forgiveness. He could be a friend for life or a lifetime enemy.

If we failed to deliver, our lives might end abruptly.

13

'Aye . . . Aye . . . Och aye. I ken youse the noo, soor, though ye've aged considerably since we last met.' Mrs Flora Crotty, proprietress of the Trotterloch Arms, had a whistling Scottish accent, but I won't attempt to reproduce much of it.

'Aged sorely, Mr Christmas, and I didn't recognize you when you came into the bar. But Time takes his toll of the best of us, and ten years' water must have flowed down the glen since you and your good lady had that wee tiff outside Sir Thomas's cottage.' Mrs Crotty had got her dates and her facts and her religious festivals wrong. It was about four years ago when Cat had tried to murder me with the carving knife, but I didn't contradict the crone. I'd hoped that she had died or lost her licence and I wouldn't have set foot inside her blasted pub if there'd been anywhere else to go.

As I'd feared, things had gone wrong soon after we left the phone box, and the snags were due to incompetence, gluttony and mechanical failure. I'd told Peg to drive, and while overtaking a bus on the motorway, she had skidded on to the central verge and burst a tyre. By the time the wheel was changed and the police had taken my particulars, Peggy complained of hunger, thirst and nervous exhaustion, and insisted that we make a detour to a motel. Half a gallon of draught Guinness had cured thirst and nerves, but two dozen oysters had made her violently sick and the journey was postponed till the next morning.

That was our first delay, but more followed and I felt like flogging the car hirer to the bone. The fan belt snapped in the Midlands and the petrol pump packed up while we were crossing into Scotland. Another night was wasted because the nearest garage had no spare in stock.

Not the last, nor the least frustration; and the final straw almost did break our backs. The nice Mr Neilsen might be growing impatient, so I drove for the rest of the way and kept my foot on the accelerator whenever possible. We made speedy progress before reaching the winding valley which guidebooks describe as Scotland's Second Glencoe . . . 'The legend-haunted . . . eagle-hovered Pass of Trotterloch', and progress down that bloody pass was even more speedy. When I transferred my foot to the brake, there was no resistance and the pedal slid smoothly to the floor. A hydraulic union had burst and only superb driving on the gears saved us. I was shaking as badly as Hurst-Hutchins when the car finally scraped alongside a kerb in the village street and stopped. My hands were still trembling while we waited for the sole mechanic in the eagle-hovered hamlet to fit a new union and bleed the brakes.

'Aye, Time's a cruel enemy, sorr. You're showing his scars, Mr Christmas, and your good leddie's filled out a bit.' Mrs Crotty placed two tots of whisky on the bar counter and studied Peg. 'Nothing wrong about that, my dear. You were a scrawny, wee thing when I first saw you with your father, and flesh suits a woman.

'And how is Sir Thomas? In good health I hope.' The old hag lacked information as well as memory and eyesight, and she clicked her tongue when Peggy answered her.

'Dead, eh! That is sad and he must be a heavy loss for you, lassie. All the village knew how close you and Sir Thomas were. More like husband and wife than father and daughter and many's the time I've seen you holding hands in yon corner.' Though Mrs Crotty was too dim-witted for sarcasm, the statement suggested that Toylar's incest notion was true, and I felt so disgusted that I squirted too much soda into my glass and spilled half the whisky.

'A sudden death, I suppose, and I wonder if Fate played a part in it. We often warned him not to sail his boat near Alt-na-Shan, and he laughed at us.' She hobbled to a window at the end of the counter and pointed at a little, rocky island on the horizon. 'Nay, he would'na land there, though. Sir Thomas might laugh, but he was no fool. He knew that Red Hand's curse on Saint Brendan lives on. He knew that it's death to set foot on that doomed island.'

Mrs Crotty raised her voice for the benefit of two quiet men reading newspapers at the back of the bar and I knew why. The said Brendan was a tenth-century Christian monk who had crossed over from Ireland to spread the good word, though to no avail. His zeal had offended an irascible chief named Mackentyre the Red Hand, and the missionary had been marooned on Alt-na-Shan to exist on shellfish and gulls' eggs. There was no knowing how long he had existed, because Mackentyre had delivered a curse on all who visited the island, and he had temporal as well as supernatural powers at his disposal. One man who defied the prohibition ended up with hands as red as Mackentyre's. The chief cut them off.

An old, romantic story which had been almost forgotten and then revived for the benefit of tourists. A sensible revival and no sensible person would wish to visit Alt-na-Shan. The island was accursed, but the curse had not been produced by any feudal chieftain. The navy, the airforce and a woman called Hilda Helmer were responsible, and the inhabitants of Trotterloch didn't discuss Miss Helmer. They valued their tourist trade and kept quiet.

'Aye, the curse of Red Hand will never be lifted, Mr Christmas.' Mrs Crotty's voice croaked loudly across the room, and then she leaned over the counter and whispered in my ear. 'But you know the truth, sorr, so don't let on, will you?' She nodded at the newspaper readers. 'Them's two Americans up for the fishin', and they might move elsewhere if they heard what really rules yon isle. The one who strides across Alt-na-Shan and will continue to stride its dead fields when you're in your grave, Mr Christmas.

'Should those Yanks ask you questions during dinner, be a good pal and repeat the old spiel about Brendan and Red Hand.'

'We won't be staying for dinner, Mrs Crotty.' I saw the door open and a gangling youth in overalls appeared. He was a man of few words, but signified that the brakes had been fixed with a thumbs-up gesture. 'We're on our way north and only called at Trotterloch to have a look at the cottage.'

'Not at this time of day, surely.' She turned to the window again, and I saw that dusk had started to fall and clouds were drifting in from the Atlantic. 'It'll be night soon, so stay here and wait till morning. Don't venture near that cottage in the dark.' Flora Crotty was a mercenary harridan, but I realized that she was not merely after the price of our bed and board. She was worried about our safety.

'See you later, gentlemen.' She smiled at the two Americans who had folded their papers and stood up, saying they fancied a short stroll before supper. 'Try to be back by seven, because the haggis will be waiting, and take your coats with you. There's more rain on the way. I can feel it in my bunions.

'Now listen to me, the pair of you.' She had waited till the door closed behind her guests and stopped smiling. 'You both know that the island curse is a lie; a trick we use to keep our tourists happy. But it's God's truth that you're going to hear now, Thomas Moscow's daughter.' She stared at Peggy and crooked a finger at the gangling mechanic. 'There's something no fey about your father's cottage, and Fergus Macadam saw it with his own eyes.

'Have a dram with the lady and gentleman and tell them what you saw, Fergus.' The lout had joined us at the bar and Mrs Crotty poured out a generous measure of malt whisky. 'Tell them why it's unwise to visit Moscow's cottage by night, Fergus. Tell them what happened to those squatters.'

'Satan's Spawn, Mr Christmas. The children of the Devil, and doubtless they're with their master now.' Fergus Macadam had appeared taciturn, but Flora Crotty's prompting and whisky supplied at my expense soon loosened his tongue and he told the story with Celtic verve and Calvinist indignation.

'They sowed the wind . . . They reaped the whirlwind . . . With these two eyes I watched them enter the pit.' Those were a few of his phrases, and though I found them humorous, the narrative confirmed my suspicions and certainly frightened Peggy. She was all for taking Mrs Crotty's advice to wait till morning and my reassurance did not cheer her. I could smell her fear as we drove to Moscow's cottage, but disregarded it. Mr Neilsen was waiting to examine our samples and I intended to deliver them to his Oban hotel that night. As Moscow's verses had stated, the treasure had a guardian who could turn flesh to stone. An objectionable lady, but I knew how to tame her, and Moscow's claims were boastful. She had failed to transform her victims into rock. She had only tortured them.

Satan's spawn . . . The Children of the Devil. Fanciful descriptions, though the squatters had been no loss to humanity. Two boys and a girl who had broken into the deserted cottage and taken up residence. Hippies and drop-outs, but harmless enough despite Fergus Macadam's righteous indignation. The boys probably shared the girl's sexual favours, and they definitely shared her money. They all smelled of reefers after her monthly allowance from some indulgent relation was paid into the bank and she made a visit to Glasgow. When the allowance was spent, they lived off the country and I couldn't see why that should have bothered Fergus. Blackberries were plentiful, rabbits crippled by myxomatosis are easily caught and dead fish could often be found on the beaches. A revolting diet and, in the coroner's opinion, insanity caused by food poisoning was responsible for their mass suicide over the cliff top. An opinion I disagreed with, and so did Fergus Macadam.

'Me lassie, Mary Campbell, and I were driving back from a dance at Liskirk, Mr Christmas, and we were both as sober as I am the noo.' He waited for Flora Crotty to pour out another Scotch at my expense; the fifth. 'Though I'm a good driver and I jammed on me brakes immediately, I well nigh hit 'em as they came across the road afore us.

'Not running or walking as humans do, sir. They was leaping and bounding like wild animals, and their faces were animal faces. I saw 'em clear in the headlamps, and it's a sight I'll no forget. Red eyes aglow, lips gaping, and hair standing up like a dog's hackles.' Fergus pulled at his whisky to deaden the unforgettable image.

'Nay, that's wrong. Not like a dog. Wolves, they were, and they howled and snarled like the wolves I've heard on the telly . . . like werewolves in a horror movie . . . like . . .' Macadam had run out of similes, but his description had given me a number of answers and I didn't begrudge him the drinks. Three blind and terrified adolescents had dashed from Moscow's cottage, and they'd howled and snarled because they were in agony. Their eyes had glowed because they were melting. Their hair had risen because something was burning it.

'Aye, leapin' and howlin' and snarlin', they was, Mr Christmas, and though me and Mary Campbell saw where they were goin', we was too afeared to try and stop 'em. We just sat and watched till they reached the cliff and went over the edge like . . .

'That's it, sir.' I'd supplied him with another simile and he nodded emphatically. 'They jumped into the sea like lemmings . . . the rats of Norway.

'And do you know why?' He paused for emphasis, and though I did know why, it's bad manners to interrupt a story, and I waited for his explanation. 'Satan dwells in that cottage and they'd raised him, Mr Christmas. They summoned the horned devil and he was behind 'em. Me and me lassie never saw him, but we knew he was there.' Macadam nodded because an even more appropriate image had struck him. 'Lucifer was driving his flock to destruction, as Our Lord drove the swine of Gadara.'

That was the end of Macadam's account, and though the coroner had scoffed at his religious solution of the mystery, I accepted the principal facts. There was a devil, but it wasn't Satan or Lucifer, and no horns were involved. The demon's name was Stethno, a local corruption of Stheno, the elder sister of Medusa the Gorgon, and snakes sprouted from her metal skull. Because the hippies had tugged at those snakes she had awakened and driven them to the cliff.

And she might drive Peggy and me after them, unless I got the sequence correct, and a magpie swooping across the road reminded me of Moscow's jingle. '. . . a black and white bird in flight . . . follow his song from left to right.'

Sir Thomas Moscow had used insane riddles because he was

insane, but the instructions in that song seemed clear enough. '*One* for sorrow – *Two* for joy – *Three* for a wedding – *Four* for a boy.' Those numerals were the key to the treasure, the only way to foil Moscow's guardian, the Princess of the Dark.

A princess who was waiting, and darkness had fallen. Alt-na-Shan was a black hump against the setting sun, and a trawler anchored out to sea looked as shadowy as a ghost ship. The mainland hills were shrouded by cloud and there was no moon or stars in the sky. The road wound and dipped through stunted pine trees and, though the headlights were on, I almost missed the turning to the cottage.

'You go alone, Bill.' Like a fool I'd told Peg what had actually happened to the hippies and I heard her teeth chatter as I stopped the car. 'I'm too scared to be any use to you, darling. My hands and feet are paralysed and I don't think I can even walk. You can manage without me, Bill, so please let me stay here.'

'You must help me, Peggy, I need you to hold the lamp.' I tried to speak with a confidence I didn't feel. 'There's no danger because we've got Moscow's combination, but I can't open the safe on my own. Forget about the squatters, Peggy, and think about the treasure. Our treasure, and Neilsen's bearer bonds.

'Yes, think about those bonds, Peggy. Just a few minutes' work and we'll be rolling in money. Think about all the furs and jewels you'll be able to buy. You'll be got up like a queen, Peg. You can ride around in a gold-plated Rolls-Royce if you want to.' By the car's interior light I saw fear and greed battling behind her eyes. 'Think how you'll be able to order servants and waiters about and lord it over everyone.'

'All right, Bill.' Peg is a bully as well as a coward and the last temptation had done the trick. She picked up the electric lantern I'd bought in the village and climbed out of the car. We walked towards the cottage which Cat and Moscow had called the House of Stethno.

I'd never liked that cottage. Even in bright sunlight and with clean paint and furnishings its atmosphere had been oppressive. Now it was chilling. One kick tore the lock from the decayed doorpost, and the living-room behind the door was a shambles.

Nobody had cleaned up after the squatters and their foulness remained. Empty bottles of cheap wine and reefer butts, ragged clothes and filthy sleeping bags, and other exhibits of human dirt too disgusting to be mentioned.

No furniture, though. Most of the items must have been sold, and the rest used for fuel. I saw a charred table leg in the grate, and even structural timbers had been ripped out and burnt. We had to cross wide gaps in the floor before I reached a stone-flagged area and looked at Moscow's Guardian.

Some classical writers and artists believed that the three Gorgons, Stheno and Euryale and Medusa, were beautiful women, apart from their snake-like hair, but Thomas Moscow had not shared that view and his image was hideous. A study of deformity which made Peggy gasp, and the deformities had been increased by the recent occupants of the house. Stethno's face was scarred with chisel marks and two of her snakes were broken. When Peg raised the lamp I saw that the serpents had been hollow tubes, and I understood everything . . . almost everything. However hideous, that iron monster was a saleable commodity and the squatters had been trying to tear Stethno from the wall when she spat her venom at them.

She would spit at me too, if I made the slightest mistake, and I consulted Moscow's instructions before starting work.

'Press the eyes which turn flesh to stone . . . Twist the snakes in the metal bone.' I raised my index fingers and forced them against the eyes. They slid smoothly back into their sockets and my spirits soared. The Gorgon's eyes were the tumblers of a lock and four of her serpents were the levers to operate it. The grotesque face was the door of a vault, and very soon that door would open and we'd see the treasure of Guido Calamai gleaming in the torchlight. Cat Guthrie's inheritance . . . Cort Neilsen's dream . . . Our ticket to El Dorado.

All I had to do was to follow the magpie rhyme from left to right, and there were no problems. Moscow's clues were so simple . . . so childish. 'One for sorrow . . . Two for joy . . .' The first and second snakes on the left moved easily. The third was stiffer, but it turned in time. The fourth was rigid and, though I told Peggy to help me and she put all her weight on that metal rod it still resisted us. We were so intent on our labours that we never heard a car draw up the lane or the footsteps crossing the garden path. We never noticed the quiet American fishermen enter the room, and we wouldn't have recognized them if we had. The cautious fellows were wearing protective masks.

We just kept straining away at the fourth lever and when it did finally move the whole monstrosity moved with it. Stethno's face swung away from the chimney and threw us to the floor. The lamp fell too, and after I regained my senses we were in darkness. I could see nothing, but I heard something, and what I heard made me clutch Peg for moral support.

'Well done, my dear.' The voice was familiar. I'd once heard it delivering a radio lecture on Etruscan architecture. The lecturer was dead . . . or supposed to have died.

'I'm extremely proud of you, Cathleen,' said Sir Thomas Moscow.

14

'You are an intelligent, devoted girl, Cathleen, and this is what you must do now.' For a moment I'd felt convinced I was listening to Moscow's ghost, but I was wrong. The voice was a mechanical recording and I didn't hear any more. Another torch lit up the room and one of the masked fishermen pushed past us and removed the record. I didn't try to stop him because his partner was armed with a submachine pistol and I lack suicidal tendencies.

Peggy and I accepted defeat gracefully, but before we were marched out of the cottage, we saw what Stethno had guarded. No treasure gleamed in the cavity in the wall. All it contained was a locking device, an old-fashioned clockwork gramophone which had been automatically switched on when the metal face swung aside, and a row of pipes and cylinders. Though we were defeated, we were lucky to be alive and my theory was correct. Those cylinders housed the demon's venom and two of them had been activated by the squatters. If I'd turned the snakes in the wrong order, their neighbours would have followed suit and we'd have had a shower bath of sulphuric acid.

My translation of Moscow's cypher had spared our lives, but what were our lives worth? The fishermen were Mr Neilsen's men. The crew of the launch which carried us out to sea were Mr Neilsen's crew. The shadowy vessel I'd thought was a trawler was Mr Neilsen's yacht; the *Midas*. The room I now sat in was Mr Neilsen's saloon. Moscow's record had become Neilsen's property, and our fellow guests were on Mr Neilsen's pay roll.

'I'm extremely pleased with you, Mr and Mrs Easter.' The compliment reminded me of Moscow's greeting to Cat, but like everything else, the words were Mr Neilsen's and he'd returned from some private sanctum to deliver good cheer. A smart, affable character with ready smile and a pair of frank, honest brown eyes. The kind of man you'd trust if you felt his hand in your pocket.

'Yes, you have both done very well. We have all the data we need now, and a celebration is the order of the day.' He nodded at a steward behind the bar. 'Bubbly please, Harry.

'I have studied Sir Thomas's recorded instructions and they are simple, precise and foolproof. Unless the weather breaks the Calamai collection should be aboard this ship by noon tomorrow.' He listened to the cheerful pop of a champagne cork and beamed at Peggy. 'Don't look so woebegone, my dear. You have had a shock and a disappointment, but there's plenty of money for everyone and I'm sure your associates will give you a fair share of the proceeds.

'In the meanwhile I would like to honour your joint courage with a toast.' The steward had passed round the glasses and he raised his own. 'Let us drink to a very gallant lady and gentleman, my dear friends.' A polite man, Mr Cort W. Neilsen, as I've said before. He drank the toast with gusto, but the dear friends were less enthusiastic. They sipped at the wine as though it was an obnoxious brand of cough mixture.

All the major conspirators were there. Booth and Lady Lesley and Hurst-Hutchins; also Cyrus Toylar, and Booth had explained their alliance. Following the fracas outside Haddock's office they had recognized each other as kindred spirits with a common aim and decided to join forces and swap information. They had also decided that we were traitors, and as I watched their expressions I knew that there'd be no rich pickings for Peggy and me. After cashing Neilsen's bonds Hurst-Hutchins would probably deliver some ecclesiastical curse against us. Booth and Lady Lesley might order their warriors to murder us. Toylar might . . .

No, I didn't want to consider what Cyrus Toylar might do if he had the chance. He hadn't believed me when I said that I'd saved his life. He was sure that I was responsible for Cat's attempt to castrate him, and though the attempt had failed he was still in obvious discomfort. He couldn't sit down and his bright, boot-polish complexion had faded to a dull, unhealthy grey. But his eyes glared with malevolence and he kept twisting his huge hands together. If those hands got hold of us, we'd die slowly and painfully.

An unpleasant quartet and Hurst-Hutchins had gloated while explaining the cause of our downfall. Toylar had retained most of the letter Moscow deposited with Haddock, and after the allies had read it, Booth's chauffeur had rushed to Healy's establishment and retrieved the second letter before the R.S.P.C.A. inspector arrived.

Armed with that information, Hurst-Hutchins had reported our treachery to Mr Neilsen, and he'd been with Neilsen when I had made my telephone call and listened in on an extension. Our arrangement to meet in Oban had set Gerry's brain cells working, because Oban is less than thirty miles from Trotterloch.

The treasure was probably hidden in Moscow's cottage and Peg and I should be encouraged to go there.

'You didn't need much encouragement, did you, Billy Boy?' Jolly Jim Jackboot took over the story from Hurst-Hutchins. 'No hard feelings about that, because you were extremely useful to us. During my enquiries into the Helmer woman's disappearance and Moscow's suicide, it was found that the Gorgon gadget had been manufactured by Moscow himself, and five pressurized cylinders of vitriol were missing from the Danemere's workshop.

'One metal mask and five cylinders of sulphuric acid – six facts which enabled me to put two and two together.' The little swine chuckled at his own wit and cleverness. 'Tom Moscow had rigged up a booby trap to protect his loot, and I decided who would be the boobies.

'We joined Mr Neilsen's yacht at Torquay and sailed to Scotland in comfort and security. You took the risks and did the dirty work for us. Not a bad piece of strategy, eh?'

Strategically, not bad, I had to agree to that, but morally despicable. If we opened the safe successfully, as we had done, Neilsen's fishermen would take over. If we'd been burned to death during the attempt, no tears would have been shed. Empty cylinders can't harm anybody and Moscow's Gorgon would have lost her venom. The fishermen could prise her from the wall in complete safety.

'Let's forget the past and plan for the future, sir.' Neilsen had seen the disgust in my face and his tone was soothing. 'A rosy future, because Sir Thomas's last message to his daughter is clear and simple, and this is where we shall find the gold.' He unrolled a map of Alt-na-Shan and pinned it to a wall board. 'As Colonel Booth told you, Moscow was friendly with a woman named Hilda Helmer, and in the year before Sir Thomas died Miss Helmer was authorized to conduct certain experiments on this island.' Neilsen produced a fountain pen from the pocket of his spruce yachtsman's jacket. 'Experiments which proved so successful that they were abandoned, and Miss Helmer lost her job. She also took her life, though that is not our concern.' He raised the pen and inked a cross on the map. 'Our concern is with Miss Helmer's laboratory, which remains intact and is located under this mountain.' He tapped the cross with a well-manicured fingernail.

'Sir Thomas Moscow's hiding place, ladies and gentlemen, and an excellent choice, though his mind was rambling towards the end. Mrs Guthrie was instructed to go there alone, but she would have needed help and equipment to retrieve the collection. The lab is located in a cave at the base of a vertical lift shaft, and the lift has been dismantled. An easy climb down, according to Sir Thomas, but the return journey would be difficult if you were burdened with half a ton of gold.

'Mrs Cathleen Guthrie would have been faced with severe problems had she attempted to follow her father's orders, but those problems will not worry us.' He paused like a company chairman informing his shareholders that there were lean times ahead, but prudence would weather the storms and reap bumper dividends.

'We have manpower and technical facilities at our disposal, and a caterpillar truck loaded with lifting tackle and other equipment is already being hoisted on to the launch which brought you here, Mr Easter.' He paused again, and a clank from outside proved that the hoisting operation was in progress.

'Most important of all, we have knowledge. Sir Thomas's record describes a locked gate at the bottom of the shaft and I have been able to work out the lock's combination, though he was a fanciful man who enjoyed riddles.

'Mrs Guthrie was told to think of William the Conqueror's invasion of England, and it's clear that the initials W.C. and the date 1066 contain the code. A simple operation, my friends, and if it were not for certain factors that Dr Toylar will explain to you, I would have liked to start work immediately. As it is, we must wait till morning and a good night's sleep will do us no harm.' He glanced at his watch, but his finger remained poised over the map. 'Any queries before we discuss technicalities, ladies and gentlemen?'

'Four questions, Mr Neilsen.' The rest of the fools had remained silent, but I voiced my queries loud and clear, because they were all important. 'Do you know what happened on Alt-na-Shan, and what is still happening there? Do you know what the local people call that island, and why they shun it like the plague?'

'Of course I do, sir, and so did Thomas Moscow. That's why he selected it as his hidey-hole, and why he instructed Cathleen Guthrie to obtain the medical protection which Dr Toylar is about to give us.' Neilsen was unimpressed by my anxiety and he smiled at Toylar who was hobbling across to a table. But I appreciate your point, Mr Easter, though *plague* is too vague a term'. He watched Toylar open a bag and bring out a rack of plastic phials.

'The local name for Alt-na-Shan is Anthrax Island.'

Everybody on the yacht had been inoculated against *Bacillus Anthrasis*, and while he pumped the serum into us Dr Toylar described the disease symptoms with relish. Fever, convulsions, and malignant pustules which swell to a great size and cause death within hours. The doctor was a fund of depressing information, but after the last jab he assured us that we'd be fully immune before daybreak and could visit the island in absolute safety. The injections would make us a bit drowsy, but as Massa Neilsen had remarked, a good night's sleep never did anyone any harm, and we could turn in without a care in the world.

Old Booth also had a lecture to deliver and he explained how Alt-na-Shan had gained its sinister reputation. Hilda Helmer had been a specialist in germ mutations and the Ministry of Defence had given her scheme *carte blanche* because it appeared more economical than normal methods of biological warfare. If an enemy's crops and live-stock could be destroyed, the resulting famine would make military action unnecessary and victory would be gained without a shot fired in anger. The foes would not even suspect the source of the epidemic. They'd go down on their knees to the country which provided an antidote.

Clever Miss Helmer worked on the anthrax bacillus in the hope of producing a strain which was harmless to human beings, but lethal to plants and animals. She vanished without revealing whether her first hope was fulfilled, but the second succeeded too well, and the authorities decided that the fun and games had to stop. The bacilli escaped from her underground lab. Alt-na-Shan died.

The soil became toxic, grass, heather and bracken withered, and the air soon stank with the rotting carcasses of birds and animals. When Miss Helmer admitted that there was no cure for the condition, she lost her job and the island was evacuated. Tests proved that, like Toylar's Disease, the contamination would remain active for almost a hundred years, and Alt-na-Shan was declared a restricted area.

The government laid on a spectacular bombardment from the sea and air and stated that the island would be used for target practice. The local people revived the Brendan myth. I'd only heard the true story because Cat must have got it from Moscow, who'd been Hilda Helmer's lover, and I hadn't really believed her till Mrs Crotty confirmed the facts after a solemn promise of secrecy. Whether or not the germs could attack human beings, their presence would have ruined Trotterloch's tourist trade, and put Flora Crotty out of business.

'Sorry if that hurt you, Mrs Tey.' Peggy had winced as Toylar jabbed her arm, but his apology was a lie. I could see that he'd enjoyed hurting her, and he'd probably used a blunt needle deliberately. He would enjoy hurting me even more if the opportunity arose, and when a steward led us to a cabin I could feel his hatred following me through the saloon door like a shadow.

A hatred which I reciprocated, and I promised myself that the opportunity would never arise, and Dr Toylar was the one to be hurt. I don't dislike blacks any more than I dislike whites, or browns, or yellows, but Cyrus Toylar was a bad black.

Black skinned and black hearted; as black as the pit we hoped to enter.

Toylar had lied in another way too. He'd said that his shots would cause drowsiness, and give us a sound night's sleep as well as protection. My pulsing bicep suggested that the serum had taken effect, but after tossing on the bunk for over three hours, I stopped trying to sleep. I felt tense and wide awake and bursting with excitement. Sleep was out of the question. There was work to be done and I could do it. A sudden brainwave had occurred to me and I got up and crossed to a port hole. When I looked out, I knew that my brainwave was a stroke of genius which couldn't fail.

The clouds had blown away. A big silver moon beamed on the water, but its rays were not as bright as my hopes. The launch was tied up below our cabin with the caterpillar truck on board, and I'd studied that launch during our journey to the ship. The hull was constructed of light plastic, so that it could be hoisted on to the *Midas* in case of emergencies, but the boat was designed as a tender which would normally be towed behind the yacht. A broad-beamed, forty-footer with bows like a landing craft's and petrol engines that had purred quietly at low revs. Their purr would increase to a roar if the revolutions were throttled up, but so what? The *Midas* was intended for comfortable long-range cruising and could probably average about eighteen or twenty knots. Over a short distance, the launch would leave her standing.

'I know what you're thinking, Bill, and I'm right with you.' Peggy had shared my sleepless excitement and joined me at the port-hole. 'As Neilsen promised we've got all the equipment we need, so what's to stop us?' She pointed to the crane on the truck, and a ramp in position by the launch's bow. 'Why don't we go now?'

'Because there are at least twenty people on this yacht, Peg, and some of them are armed.' I might have been elated, but I wasn't insane. 'Before we do anything I want to know if they're capable of using their guns, so let's find out.'

We dressed and tiptoed quietly out of the cabin, but there was no need for silence. When I'd first seen the *Midas*, she had made me think of a ghost ship manned by a dead crew, and the image returned because its occupants were dead to the world. Toylar had failed to put us to sleep, but everyone else was sleeping, and each door we opened told the same story.

Hurst-Hutchins snoring as hoggishly as the hog he was. Mr Neilsen lying in his stateroom like the stone statue of a Roman emperor. Booth and Lady Lesley, who had been given a double bed, positioned themselves as far away from each other as space permitted before drowsing off.

Understandable modesty, and the less modest exhibitions didn't bother me. The bar steward and one of the fishermen locked in a homosexual embrace. Toylar, stark naked with teeth grinning like a saw rasping through dry timber. Nothing could bother me, and I was so light-hearted that I never wondered why Peg and I had escaped the clutches of Morpheus. After collecting Neilsen's map from the saloon, I kissed Peggy and we laughed aloud.

Things were going so well, that once again I imagined God had joined forces with us. Before the sleepers awakened, Guido Calamai's treasure would be aboard the launch. Before they realized the launch was missing, we'd be on our way to the Clyde, where I had an acquaintance in the jewellery business. Before the day was out, Mr Cort W. Neilsen would receive a message on his ship-to-shore radio.

If C.W.N. wanted the treasure he could have it. But there would be no bishops or colonels or bogus anglers in attendance when the deal was completed.

We'd meet alone, though in a public place. Under the clock at Glasgow Central Station, and Mr Neilsen had better bring the bearer bonds with him. A single false move and Neilsen could say goodbye to his dinner service. It would be melted down by my jeweller pal and end up as medallions, wedding rings and other trinkets.

So easy – so simple and foolproof. As simple as Tom Moscow's cypher, and when Peggy suggested we should knock a hole in the yacht's lifeboat, I told her not to bother. I was so convinced that we wouldn't be followed and I wanted to get my hands on that gold without delay. We climbed into the launch, released the mooring ropes and waited for the tide to carry us away from M.V. *Midas*. Once the launch was clear, I started the engines and we set off.

Off to Aladdin's cave . . . off to Alt-na-Shan . . . off to Anthrax Island.

15

Alt-na-Shan is a plateau surrounded by steep cliffs, and a mountain rising from the centre of the plateau produces the hump-like appearance I'd seen from the mainland. A small mountain, less than a thousand feet high, and the cliffs do not exceed three hundred feet. But they looked enormous and unclimbable in the moonlight, and even with Neilsen's map it took us some time to find the single landing place: a narrow, sandy beach with a gully behind it.

There had once been a wooden jetty, but most of the timbers had been burned when the research project was abandoned, though the supporting posts remained and I suspected they'd been left as navigational hazards to discourage visitors. The blackened stumps could have crushed our hull, and I had to concentrate hard to edge the launch past them on to the sand.

'DANGER . . . KEEP OUT . . . NAVAL FIRING RANGE.' Though the last statement was untrue, the warnings were prominently displayed on notice-boards of rust-proof alloy, and each board was topped by a skull and cross bones device. The barbed-wire fence screening the gully was also rust-free, but Mr Neilsen had kept his promise and all the necessary equipment was available. While I lowered the landing ramp, Peggy attacked the fence with a pair of wire cutters, and the road was open when I drove the truck on to the beach.

Road was not a boastful description. A tarmac lane ran through the valley, and though time and weather and neglect had taken their toll, there had been no human sabotage. The authorities had stupidly decided that their notices and wire were sufficient deterrents, but they were wrong. Our vehicle lumbered up to the plateau without difficulty.

The difficulties started when we reached the plateau, because the tarmac had crumbled in places and it had been a wet autumn. The caterpillar tracks churned through mud and pools of water and once or twice it seemed as though we were bogged down for good.

But I somehow knew that that wasn't possible, and so did Peggy. Though the machine might sink and founder at times, our spirits remained as high as ever and we never doubted that those slipping tracks would eventually bite into rock or firm ground and carry us out of the marsh. They always did, and before long the earth became hard and dry and the road pointed like an arrow towards the mountain. As we rumbled on, Peg started to croon 'The Bonny Banks of Loch Lomond', but I scarcely heard her. My senses were searching for other things, and I soon realized those things didn't exist.

The bog had not smelled of decay as marshland normally does and there was no scent of heather or any other plant life. No animal life was present either. Not a single sheep was grazing on the plateau. No rabbits or hares darted before the head lamps, no gulls screamed over the cliffs, no land birds rose from the few stunted trees flanking the mountain.

Nor did the trees stir in the little breeze blowing in from the sea. Their branches were too rigid to move, because there was no sap in them. The bog was odourless because it had been poisoned. The animals were silent and motionless because they were dead, and here and there I could see skeletons lying white in the moonlight.

With the exception of ourselves and one companion, Alt-na-Shan was deserted, and I prayed that Toylar's serum proved effective. Our companion's name was *Bacillus Anthrasis*, and he was King of the Castle.

'This must be it, Peg.' The road had reached an expanse of concrete and I looked at a battlefield. The third warning notice had not been entirely false, and after the research project was abandoned the navy and the R.A.F. had had an hour's fun. Three brick buildings were in ruins and the area was pitted with craters. A derrick and a lift cage marked the shaft of the cave, but they were rusting and shattered, and a shell had scooped out a section of the cliff looming above them. The resulting overhang looked as though a strong wind might produce an avalanche, and scree lay everywhere. For the first time since we decided to leave our buddies on the yacht I felt deflated. Miss Helmer's underground lab must be blocked by rubble, and falling rocks had crushed Moscow's treasure.

As it happened, I was wrong. In retrospect I often wish I'd been right.

. . . . .

'Are you ready, Bill?' I'd put on an anorak and a miner's crash helmet fitted with a lamp and a telephone, and Peggy spoke as urgently as Gretchen Schmidt had done before shoving me out of the helicopter. But I didn't need a push this time. The shaft leading to the cave was open, and though it looked black and menacing, I was eager to go.

What had I got to fear? The truck was securely chocked with stones and its crane jib was poised over the shaft. The winch motor was running smoothly, and the winch operated two drums and two cables. One of the cables had already lowered a weighted nylon net into the cave, and with any luck that net would soon be stuffed with Calamai's creations and bearing them back to the surface. The second cable supported a bos'n's chair and a formidable tool kit to deal with the snags I might encounter. An acetylene torch to cut open the lab door if its lock had corroded. A pick and shovel to remove any rock falls which blocked my way. Three sticks of plastique explosive in case the blockages were really severe.

Mr Neilsen had provided me with all the materials I needed, but my personal assets were more important. I had courage and absolute self-confidence, and no treasure hunter could ask for more. I was also convinced that the Almighty had blessed our enterprise, and I raised a hand to salute His star-spangled heavens as I stepped into the chair and told Peg to lower away.

In a normal frame of mind, I would have found the descent unnerving. The shaft was a natural fissure, but man had widened it in places and laid obstacles. The rusty frame of the lift seemed to claw at me as I swung round in the seat, and at one point I jammed my foot against the rail and had to shout into the phone for Peggy to stop the winch till I freed myself. That was when I was about a third of the way down, and the weighted sack had proved that the floor of the cave was over four hundred feet from the surface. A chilling journey, but it didn't bother me, and after Peggy told me I'd reached the half-way mark, I sang a couple of passages from Housman's *Shropshire Lad*:

Come you home a hero,
Or come not home at all,
The lads you leave will mind you
Till Ludlow tower shall fall.

I didn't give a cuss whether the Ludlow louts minded me, and their tower could fall as soon as it liked for all I cared. But I intended to come home a hero, and more than a hero. Before long I'd be a millionaire and I bellowed the next verse with added fervour,

And you will list the bugle
That blows in winds of morn,
And make the foes of England
Be sorry you were born.

Nor did I care about the foes of England, but my own foes would regret my birth, and I made a pleasant decision. After cashing Mr Neilsen's bonds, I'd write a letter to the Director of Public Prosecutions telling him to examine the so-called Danemere collection and look into the affairs of Messrs Booth and C.W.N. I'd also tell the Leonian authorities that Gerry Hurst-Hutchins was at large, and plotting their downfall.

And you will list the bugle
That blows in lands of morn . . .

I repeated the lines and then broke off abruptly. I'd listed something, and it wasn't a bugle or the echo of my voice against the rocks. The sound was coming from below and growing louder yard by yard. A sobbing, moaning sound which made me think of ghosts and banshees, and men and women dying in agony. A sickening sound that deflated my confidence and raised several sickening notions. I was on the point of telling Peg to reverse the winch, when I saw the source of the noise and laughed at my fears.

The banshee is an Irish superstition, and Saint Brendan's ghost had been laid generations ago. Hilda Helmer was dead, and so were Thomas Moscow and all his fellow victims of Calamai's curse. They'd killed themselves to escape mania and torture, and there was no human life or supernatural force at work in the cave. No ghosts or human beings could harm me, but something else could. Something which was very much alive, and before reaching the floor of the cave I twisted out of the way of a naked old-fashioned electric knife-switch.

The cave was as big as a medium-sized church and it resembled a church. The ceiling and walls were fluted with limestone deposits, and a cluster of stalactites sprouted from one corner like organ pipes. In front of the cluster stood the organ itself. A vast, black cylinder booming out a song which might continue interminably unless there was a severe drought on the island or a bearing failed.

My banshee was a water-powered dynamo and a row of dials proved that its current was flowing freely. I couldn't imagine why it hadn't been destroyed or dismantled with the rest of Miss Helmer's apparatus. Probably no volunteer had been prepared to venture down the tunnel, but I didn't consider the question closely. My sole concern was to get at the gold before our sleeping comrades on the *Midas* awakened, and the dynamo should prove a much more reliable friend and comrade. It was certainly a less dormant ally, and when I pulled the knife-switch there was a greenish flicker across the roof and a dozen incandescent lights blazed into activity. The cavern became as bright as a Mediterranean beach in summer and almost as noisy.

My demand for more power had increased the dynamo's revs and its whine became so loud that I could barely hear Peg's voice on the telephone. She was saying something about a plane but Alt-na-Shan lies under one of the North Atlantic routes, and I didn't know why a low-flying airliner should worry her so I switched off the set. Our only worry was to open the vault and remove the gold and, apart from one slight difficulty, the problems were solved. The nylon net was in position, the steel door leading to the inner chamber was visible on the far wall and I could see two more dials beside it.

The difficulty arose when I walked towards those dials. Like the squatters, I became blind.

A frightening affliction, but easily cured after I realized that the cave was not merely as bright and noisy as a Mediterranean beach. Its atmosphere was stifling hot and sweat had fogged-up the visor of the helmet. As soon as I'd removed the visor, my sight returned and the cause of the heat wave became apparent. The dynamo was driving a refrigerating plant, and a machine resembling an enormous motor radiator was connected to the inner cavern.

I suppose that should have warned me, but it didn't. I rushed to the door like a drunk trying to reach a pub before closing time, and I scarcely glanced at the first of the dials. If I had, I'd have seen that the thing was an electric clock set to release the locking mechanism in ninety-seven years' time. The expected life-span of Miss Helmer's anthrax mutation. The probable span of something else which I'd almost forgotten.

I'd forgotten damn near everything, except the name of a king and the best-known date in British history. William the Conqueror . . . the Norman invasion. Tom Moscow's final clue.

'W. C. 1 0 6 6.' The numbered disc revolved as smoothly as

Hurst-Hutchins's conscience. The heavy steel barrier rose as arrogantly as Lady Lesley's eyebrows. A blast of icy air stabbed me as painfully as Cat Guthrie's knife.

I looked at the treasure of Guido Andrea Calamai.

16

Calamai's original creations were displayed on a marble-topped table a few yards from the door and they looked far less impressive than the Danemere's pinchbeck replicas. Each piece had a grey, anaemic tinge; more like pewter than gold, and at first I thought that Moscow had played a cruel practical joke on Cat and I'd found a second set of fakes. After I reached out to pick up the nearest item, the same tainted chalice which had housed the spores, I ceased to think. I yelped.

The stem of the cup felt as though it was white-hot and pain made rational thought impossible. I couldn't think and I couldn't let go. My hand seemed to be glued to the metal figurine of Polyphemus and the goblet itself was glued to the marble. Glued by frozen moisture, though I didn't realize that for a while. The inner cavern was a vast ice-box and frost had produced the leaden hue on the gold.

And though the fridge was warming up, I didn't notice the changing temperature as fans activated by the dial drove gusts of hot air into the open chamber. I didn't hear the fans and I didn't look around the room or consider why it had been constructed and what else it contained. I didn't see anything except that damned cup which was searing my flesh, and I didn't hear anything except my own voice cursing the torture of frostbite. I just struggled to free myself and I almost failed. My muscles were paralysed and, when I finally pulled the goblet away from the table and staggered back, it was still clenched in my fingers.

But after I reached the doorway, I did see, I did hear and I did think. I understood the lot, and the realization made me forget pain. Nothing would surprise me any more, and my reason returned as I climbed into the bos'n's chair, switched on the helmet microphone, and told Peggy to haul me up very slowly. I wasn't even surprised when a male voice acknowledged the demand, because I knew what had happened.

The sleepers were awake, and we'd got company.

'That is the truth, Mr Easter?' Cort Neilsen was waiting at the top of the shaft, and though he smiled as jovially as ever, his tension was apparent. 'All you found was a strong room containing the treasure, which you have loaded into the net?'

'I've just told you so.' During the ascent I'd regained more composure and tried to sound calm, but irritable. 'Your bloody dinner service is ready for collection and all you have to do is wind it up.' I stepped out of the chair and pointed at the winch. 'What's stopping you?'

'Self-preservation, sir, but your manner suggests that our anxieties are groundless.' He turned to the other members of the welcoming committee; Booth and Toylar, Lady Lesley and Gretchen Schmidt. A formidable combination and Lady L. had a pistol jammed against Peggy's spine. Though I'd stuffed one of the plastique charges into my jacket there was no chance of using it then and there. Lies were my only trump cards and I watched our enemies' expressions as Neilsen questioned them. 'Do you agree, ladies and gentlemen?'

'I certainly do, so let's get on with it.' Colonel Jack acted as spokesman, and, apart from Toylar, the rest of them nodded. The doctor was still unconvinced by my report and he stood with an ear cocked over the shaft. 'We know that Mr Easter is a liar, and he may also be unobservant. I think we should wait till there is more light, Colonel Booth.'

'Stuff and nonsense, Doctor. I'm not waiting any longer.' Booth dismissed the objection and crossed to the truck. 'For once in his deceitful life, Mr Easter is telling the truth, and our ruse was unnecessary.' He put the second winch drum into gear and grinned mockingly at me. 'Unnecessary, though clever, Billy Boy. The immunization shots Dr Toylar gave you and Peggy contained benzedrine; a drug which produces courage and false security.

'That's what made you decide to cheat us again, but the injections we received did not cause drowsiness, as you imagined. We were all wide awake when you visited our cabins, and as soon as you'd left the yacht, I radioed a message to Fräulein Schmidt, who was waiting on the mainland to fetch us.' He waved his heavy Webley revolver at the *Midas* silhouetted against the rising sun, and then at an aircraft parked on the tarmac road. The same helicopter that had rescued Cat Guthrie from the asylum. The plane that Peggy was reporting when I switched off the telephone. 'Any idea why the ruse was required, Bill?'

'We're not imbeciles, you pocket Napoleon.' Though I was scared stiff, the play had to go on and my display of anger was impressive. 'You thought that Moscow might have devised more mechanical guardians to protect his hoard. Vitriol sprays or a bomb which would explode if the safe combination was wrong. As usual I was to be on the receiving end while you sat on your cowardly arses in safety.'

'Dead right, my boy, and I'm afraid that *end* and *dead* are the operative words.' The little sadist watched the cable sliding through the crane block. 'You and Peggy took the risks, we're about to reap the benefits of your labours, and you are both expendable now. Tom Moscow's store house will be your grave, and my sole regret is that Gerald Hurst-Hutchins is not with us to administer the last rites.' He laughed and waved his gun at the helicopter again.

'Sad for him and tragic for you. Gerry's weight was the drawback because the chopper has a limited load capacity, and with the gold on board, we'll have no room for passengers.

'Don't despair for your souls, however. I'm certain the bishop is with you in spirit and our employer is a minister of the Unitarian Church.' He smiled at Neilsen. 'Will you give them decent burials, C.W.N.?'

'Brief burials, Colonel, because I've got a hunch that there's a storm on the way.' Though Neilsen was fascinated by the revolving winch drum he kept glancing up at the sky. 'One hell of a storm.'

He could be right. People like Cort Wilhelm Neilsen usually are right, and though dawn was breaking, the sunrise had a pale, unhealthy look about it – as pallid and sickly as the treasure had looked in its iced lacquer; and the mountain above us was shrouded by cloud.

I'm not a religious man and I hated Mr Neilsen, but I prayed for him at that moment. If his weather forecast was correct, we had a chance of survival. He would die . . . We might live.

His forecast *was* correct. The net attached to the cable was nearly half-way home when the first flash of lightning flickered and the whirr of the winch was drowned by thunder. Rain followed immediately and it was exactly the kind of rain I'd hoped for. Heavy, leaden drops which bounced from the concrete like ping-pong balls and almost blinded us.

Almost, but not quite. Gretchen had produced a torch and its beam was directed on the cable. The thin wire line bringing in the goods . . . retrieving Moscow's stolen hoard from its ice-bound vault . . . winding Calamai's masterpieces up through the shaft . . . up to the friendly bosom of Mother Earth . . . up to save us.

'Show me your hand, Easter.' Booth and Neilsen and Gretchen were craning over the pit, and though Lady Lesley's gun still covered Peggy she shared their excitement. But Cyrus Toylar was a physician and a psychologist and an observant fellow. He'd seen that my fingers were swollen, he still suspected I was acting, and he stepped towards me.

'The other one, you fool.' I'd held out my uninjured left hand and he reached for the right. What he saw made him swing round to tell Booth to stop the winch, but no words came. My foot caught him in the exact spot Cat's knife had opened and he toppled against Lady L. knocking the pistol from her grasp.

Though they both screamed and cursed, only Peggy and I heard them. Thunder muted the cries and their companions were too preoccupied to notice the commotion. As I'd promised, the sack had been loaded and the next flash of lightning revealed the gold. Guido Calamai's treasure was up. Our partners were about to go down.

A well-guarded treasure, but its guardians were not mechanical devices. They were alive . . . alive and kicking.

I think that Booth and Gretchen fired two shots, but I can't be certain. What I do remember is the expression on Neilsen's face, when he dragged in the net and realized that it had brought more than metal to the surface.

Things were clinging to the nylon mesh. The same deformed, fungoid things I'd seen in the cave, but far more horrible and a hundred times more active. They'd been weak and bewildered when heat melted their icy shrouds and they staggered from the floor and moved towards me. I wasn't sure whether they'd heard my promise to haul them up with their treasure, but I need not have worried. They had heard what I said as I rose above them. They'd heard, they'd understood, and they had not only regained strength and intelligence; they were in agony.

An anguish which produced hatred, though I didn't stop to watch the results of their fury. I grabbed Peggy's wrist and we ran across the concrete as though the devil was after us, as indeed he was. When I finally turned and looked back, the Booths and Toylar and Neilsen and Gretchen were all dead and their executioners had started to walk towards us. Walking slowly, but purposefully, and I saw the leader's features clearly as I pulled out the plastique charge and set the detonator.

'Hail and farewell, Sir Thomas Moscow,' I said and lobbed the bomb at him.

Postscript

'Stop it, Peggy.' The danger was past, the storm had blown away, and the sun was shining. I'd explained everything to Peg, but she was still crouched against a boulder and sobbing with what I imagined to be craven terror.

'Stop crying, woman.' Though I'd missed my target, the job was completed and far more effectively than I had hoped. The plastique had overshot Moscow and exploded against the cliff, which was weak and crumbling and poised to fall. The ensuing avalanche had plunged forward into the mine shaft and carried a great many things with it. The truck and the crane and nine bodies. Five human corpses and four half-human monsters. 'They're all dead and buried, Peggy, and you've got nothing to cry about.'

'Haven't I, Bill?' She finally raised her face from the rock and I saw that fear wasn't responsible for the emotional display. 'Oh, God, why did I have to be lumbered with a fool like you, Bill? A brainless, cowardly cretin, whose panic has cost us a fortune.

'Just look what you've done.' She stalked back to the blocked shaft and I followed her in bewilderment and anger. Though Peggy lacks the quality of gratitude I'd saved the fat bitch's life and I hadn't expected abuse.

'Were you blind, Bill? Couldn't you see that they were dying when you threw that bomb at them? Killing Booth and the others was their last effort and the germs would have stopped them without your senseless massacre.' Her rage echoed around the mountain, but I didn't say a word in my defence. Peggy was right and I had no defence to offer.

Moscow and Miss Helmer and their friends had experimented with Calamai's poison spores and contracted a horrible disease. To avoid agony and the isolation ward, they had feigned suicide and locked themselves away on Alt-na-Shan. Their hope was that intense cold would preserve their bodies in suspended animation and halt the illness till a cure was found or until the bacillus completed its hundred-year life-cycle and died. If the first happened, Cat Guthrie, who had been deliberately infected, would release them and bring the antidote with her. If Cat was not cured the time lock would open the door automatically.

Up to a point the plan was successful. The sleepers had lain dormant, but the germs had not slept. The disease flourished in the ice and was approaching its terminal stage when I entered the cave and warm air revived the victims.

A brief revival, and as Peg had said, the escape and the effort of killing Neilsen and his employees had been too strenuous. My bomb had destroyed harmless, dying invalids and buried our fortune.

'Of course I'm right, Bill. I usually am right, and you're always wrong.' I'd admitted my error when we reached the rock fall, but Peggy was in no mood for apologies and her tears dribbled into the rubble. 'The shaft is blocked. The treasure is lost for ever, and we've got nothing. We've gained nothing at all, and after all the agony I've suffered . . . All the persecution and . . .'

'You mean the agony I suffered, Peg.' My hand was throbbing painfully, but I didn't care. The pain reminded me of an item I'd completely forgotten and I was about to reveal the exhibit before thinking better of it. There wasn't enough for the two of us and, as the poet said, 'He travels the fastest who travels alone.' I intended to travel without Mrs Margaret Tey in the future and the thing in my anorak would enable me to travel a long way.

Not a fortune, but a nice nest egg, and the prize of Guido Calamai's collection. The little Cyclops goblet which had started the ball rolling.

ALSO AVAILABLE FROM VALANCOURT BOOKS

Michael Arlen	Hell! said the Duchess
R. C. Ashby (Ruby Ferguson)	He Arrived at Dusk
Frank Baker	The Birds
Charles Beaumont	The Hunger and Other Stories
Charles Birkin	The Smell of Evil
John Blackburn	A Scent of New-Mown Hay
	Broken Boy
	Blue Octavo
	The Flame and the Wind
	Nothing but the Night
	Bury Him Darkly
	Our Lady of Pain
	The Household Traitors
	The Face of the Lion
	A Beastly Business
	The Bad Penny
Thomas Blackburn	A Clip of Steel
	The Feast of the Wolf
Jack Cady	The Well
R. Chetwynd-Hayes	The Monster Club
Basil Copper	The Great White Space
	Necropolis
Frank De Felitta	The Entity
Barry England	Figures in a Landscape
Ronald Fraser	Flower Phantoms
Gillian Freeman	The Liberty Man
	The Leather Boys
	The Leader
Stephen Gilbert	The Landslide
	The Burnaby Experiments
	Ratman's Notebooks
Stephen Gregory	The Cormorant
Thomas Hinde	The Day the Call Came
Claude Houghton	I Am Jonathan Scrivener
	This Was Ivor Trent
James Kennaway	The Mind Benders
Gerald Kersh	Fowlers End
	Nightshade and Damnations

Hilda Lewis	The Witch and the Priest
John Lodwick	Brother Death
Michael McDowell	The Amulet
	The Elementals
Beverley Nichols	Crazy Pavements
Oliver Onions	The Hand of Kornelius Voyt
J.B. Priestley	Benighted
	The Doomsday Men
	The Other Place
	The Magicians
	Saturn Over the Water
	The Thirty-First of June
	The Shapes of Sleep
	Salt Is Leaving
Forrest Reid	Following Darkness
	The Spring Song
	Brian Westby
	The Tom Barber Trilogy
	Denis Bracknel
George Sims	Sleep No More
	The Last Best Friend
Andrew Sinclair	The Facts in the Case of E.A. Poe
	The Raker
Colin Spencer	Panic
David Storey	Radcliffe
Michael Talbot	The Delicate Dependency
Russell Thorndike	The Slype
	The Master of the Macabre
John Trevena	Sleeping Waters
John Wain	Hurry on Down
	The Smaller Sky
	Strike the Father Dead
	A Winter in the Hills
Hugh Walpole	The Killer and the Slain
Keith Waterhouse	There is a Happy Land
	Billy Liar
Colin Wilson	Ritual in the Dark
	Man Without a Shadow
	The World of Violence
	The Philosopher's Stone
	The God of the Labyrinth

WHAT CRITICS ARE SAYING ABOUT VALANCOURT BOOKS

'Valancourt are doing a magnificent job in making these books not only available but – in many cases – known at all . . . these reprints are well chosen and well designed (often using the original dust jackets), and have excellent introductions.'

Times Literary Supplement (London)

'Valancourt Books champions neglected but important works of fantastic, occult, decadent and gay literature. The press's Web site not only lists scores of titles but also explains why these often obscure books are still worth reading. . . . So if you're a real reader, one who looks beyond the bestseller list and the touted books of the moment, Valancourt's publications may be just what you're searching for.'

Michael Dirda, *Washington Post*

'Valancourt Books are fast becoming my favourite publisher. They have made it their business, with considerable taste and integrity, to put back into print a considerable amount of work which has been in serious need of republication. If you ever felt there were gaps in your reading experience or are simply frustrated that you can't find enough good, substantial fiction in the shops or even online, then this is the publisher for you.'

Michael Moorcock